MW00573399

This special signed edition of

JOHNNY HALLOWEEN:

Tales of the Dark Season

is limited to 1,500 copies.

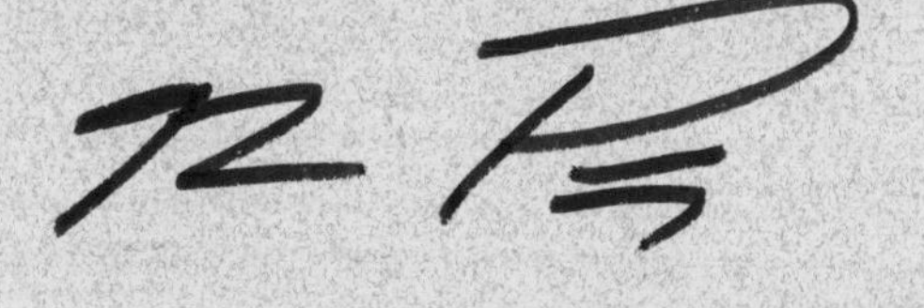

JOHNNY HALLOWEEN:

Tales of the Dark Season

JOHNNY HALLOWEEN:

Tales of the Dark Season

NORMAN PARTRIDGE

CEMETERY DANCE PUBLICATIONS

Baltimore

❖ 2010 ❖

Cemetery Dance Publications
132-B Industry Lane, Unit #7
Forest Hill, MD 21050
http://www.cemeterydance.com

First Limited Edition Printing

ISBN-13: 978-1-58767-223-1
ISBN-10: 1-58767-223-5

Interior Design by Kate Freeman Design

This one's for Minh Nguyen.
May your treat bag always be full, pard!

TABLE OF CONTENTS

INTRODUCTION:
Dark Seasons Past

My first memories of Halloween are the monsters. Frankenstein, Dracula, the Wolf Man...you can toss in the Mummy, too. We're talking early sixties here, when the Universal Studios creepers reigned over the popular culture landscape—one they'd dominated, at that point, for more than thirty years.

I cut my imaginative teeth on those movies, and then I went looking for more stuff that would provide the same kind of thrill. It was a good time to do that, because the late sixties and early seventies marked a golden age for young horror fans. Monster culture had trickled down into kid culture in a big way, and not just in film and television. *Famous Monsters* magazine was easily found at the local bottle shop (my mom's polite parental euphemism for "liquor store"). Bill Warren's black & white horror comics, *Creepy* and *Eerie*, had taken the place of the EC Comics horror line—right down to their cackling horror host characters. Paperback anthologies featuring classic horror stories were plentiful and cheap in creaky turnstile racks.

If kids wanted more, they could even get up-close-and-personal with their favorite horrors. Head down to the local hobby shop and you could buy Aurora monster model kits for just under a buck, featuring the Universal standbys and a few others to boot. Grab one of those kits and some Testors paints, and you were in business. If it was the right time of year, you might even hear "The Monster Mash" blaring from the local Top 40 station while you turned your bedroom into a glow-in-the-dark Chamber of Horrors.

Needless to say, that's exactly what I did. I had all the Aurora monster models on my bookcases—at least until I got my Daisy BB gun and they turned into targets. The day after the grand shootout, I moped around like an impulsive dictator who'd lined up his best friends against a brick wall and executed them—which I admit is a metaphor that really pushes the envelope, but I hope you'll indulge it because I really did feel that way. Add to that weekly viewings of Bob Wilkins' *Creature Features* on television, and a couple of Super-8mm monster movies to my name,[1] and I guess that made me a card-carrying *monsterkid.*

That's the *term du jour* for monster lovers from the Boomer generation. Many years have passed since then, but I still love that stuff. Admittedly, there's more than a little nostalgia mixed in with that love, plus what I like to think of as the thrill of the original scare.

Let me explain that last part. It's my opinion that the strongest horror experiences are our first ones—and that's why each generation of writers points to different touchstones with equal enthusiasm. So while writers younger than me might reference zombies in a variety of media, music videos like Michael Jackson's "Thriller," and horror movie remakes of seventies

1 *The Ghoul* was about five minutes long and had a body count three times that. *Dracula vs. the Wolf Man* was a love letter to the Universal gang.

grindhouse fare, my particular touchstones remain the Universal monsters, Rod Serling's *Twilight Zone* and *Night Gallery*, and the group of writers I like to think of as the California Sorcerers. And—surprise, surprise—I've found that most writers my age mention exactly the same influences when asked.

Not to say movies like *Night of the Living Dead* and seventies drive-in horror movies didn't influence me, too, but those came later. Like I said, the work that bites first bites hardest. Pre-*NOTLD* movies, TV, and comics were my very first horror experiences. It took me awhile to find the real-deal books. But when I did graduate from the ghost story anthologies and the Alfred Hitchcock compendiums I found in the kid's section of the library, I couldn't have encountered a better group of teachers than the aforementioned sorcerers from California: Ray Bradbury, Robert Bloch, Richard Matheson, and Charles Beaumont. As I grew older, several paperback crime writers joined them. They all left distinctive marks on my imagination.

So did Halloween, of course. The holiday had its own set of original scares for me. Even today, memories of my early Octobers seem stronger, more vibrant somehow. Like carving pumpkins with my dad's jackknife (I've still got a zigzag scar on my thumb to prove it).[2] Or taking days to plan a costume, or weeks to build a horror display with my buddies.

One year we built a cemetery in my front yard. It certainly wasn't the kind of thing you'd plop down money for at a Halloween Superstore—my dad made our half-buried coffin out of leftover fence boards, and our headstones were scrap wood cut-to-order on his table-saw and hand-painted by my friends and I. But we thought it was great, and so did most of the kids in the neighborhood. Hey, we even had a looted grave complete with unearthed corpse. I, of course, was the live-action ghoul

2 My old man didn't believe in stitches. He believed in cotton and that sticky white medical tape...lots of it.

digging the guy up—which always seemed to me a particularly terrifying creature to be, and one of the creepiest endeavors I could imagine *undertaking.*[3]

When it comes to the stories in this collection, I'd have to say I haven't changed much. Certain things still give me the chills. Like cemeteries. There are a lot of those in my stories, and some pretty disturbing monsters inhabit them. Some are supernatural, and some are human—and that leads to another Halloween experience that helped shape me as a writer.

I'm talking about Halloween 1969, when I was eleven years old. That was the year I realized that the scariest monsters wore human skin, and the realization didn't have anything to do with the fictional creatures I read about or watched on television. The monster in question lived right in my blue-collar hometown, a San Francisco Bay Area suburb by the name of Vallejo.

Vallejo had two claims to fame in those days: 1) a naval shipyard that turned out nuclear submarines, and 2) the nation's first modern-day serial killer: the Zodiac. I won't say too much about the Zodiac here—you'll get a much fuller picture in "The Man Who Killed Halloween," an essay included in this book—but I will say that the Zodiac's crimes had a strong impact on me. He taught me about a new kind of fear. One that didn't have anything to do with creatures that went bump in the night, or the roller-coaster rides they took me on in movies or comics or stories contained neatly between hard covers.

By then I understood those monsters. I knew their secrets, their strengths and weaknesses. More importantly, they were easy to recognize. But the Zodiac was different. There were no bolts in his neck requiring periodic recharging. He didn't sleep in a coffin by day, powerless, afraid of the sun. No pentagram marked his palm. No. Looking at that old police artist's

3 Hey, I've mentioned Robert Bloch and Uncle Creepy in this introduction. You've got to allow me one bad pun.

depiction of the killer today, I still recognize the thing I saw when I looked at the front page of *The Vallejo Times-Herald* and confronted that artist's rendering for the first time. His was the face of a very human monster—without a doubt containing a cancerous growth of evil, and at the same time not evidencing a single cell of that particular disease on the surface.

I couldn't have articulated that perception then, but that's exactly the way the Zodiac's picture struck me. It strikes me the same way today. He didn't look at all like a monster, though that's exactly what he was. His face was like the faces of a half-dozen fathers who lived in my very own neighborhood, right down to the horn-rim glasses. He could have been sitting at a breakfast table down the block, eating Corn Flakes while I stared at his picture on the front page. And that sudden realization broke down something very simple for me: *the Zodiac could walk among us, and no one would know they needed to fear him until it was MUCH TOO LATE.*

That was one of the most terrifying revelations of my youth, and I remember it to this day. It changed the way I saw people. It changed the way I thought. If you've read my Halloween novel, *Dark Harvest*, you know it made a mark on my fiction, too... and a pretty big one. It influenced several of the stories you're about to read, as well.

Of course, the other stuff did, too—those original scares from movies and comics and television. I still love them, and I still love Halloween, too. These days, my bride and I stretch it into a month-long celebration. For us, the holiday is mostly about the fun stuff. We uncrate the old-fashioned Halloween kitsch and decorate the living room. We get an early jump watching those classic Universal creepers. We eat lots of home-popped popcorn. And when the big day comes I always carve a couple of pumpkins, which may seem a dangerous tradition given my past history. But, hey—the good news is that I haven't sliced open my thumb in years.

But it doesn't take much to stir those deeper fears, even today. The ones first planted by a serial killer who blended in so well he was never caught. Once the celebration is over and the quiet of another fall night settles in, it's the simple things that creep me out. Like the kid in the mask who's too old to be knocking on our door—the one who comes late and stands there just a little too long, staring, after I've dropped candy into his bag. Or the car that lingers in front of the house when I step outside to blow out the flickering candles in those Jack o' Lanterns. Or the sound in the backyard in the shank of the night—the one I can't identify, the one I shouldn't have heard at all.

Yeah. That's the stuff that really gives me the creeps.

And that's why I always keep one eye on the shadows.

Fact is, I found these stories there.

I hope they scare you…and good.

—Norman Partridge
Lafayette, California

JOHNNY HALLOWEEN

I should have never been there.

Number one: I was off duty. Number two: even though I'm the sheriff, I believe in letting my people earn their pay. In other words, I don't follow them around with a big roll of toilet paper waiting to wipe their asses for them, even when it comes to murder cases. And number three: I'm a very sound sleeper—generally speaking, you've got a better chance of finding Elvis Presley alive than you've got of waking me between midnight and six.

But it was Halloween, and the kids next door were having a loud party, and I couldn't sleep. Sure, I could have broken up the party, but I didn't. I'm a good neighbor. I like to hear the sound of kids having fun, even if I think the music we listened to back in the fifties was a lot easier on the ears. So I'm not sour on teenagers, like some cops. Probably has something to do with the fact that Helen and I never had any kids of our own.

It just didn't work out for us, is all. When Helen had the abortion, we were young and stupid and we figured we'd have plenty of chances later on. That wasn't the way it worked out, though. I guess timing is everything. The moment passes, things change, and the life you thought you'd have isn't there when you catch up to it.

What it is, is you get older. You change and you don't even notice it. You think you're making the decisions, but mostly life is making them for you. You're just along for the ride. Reacting, not acting. Most of the time you're just trying to make it through another day.

That's how most cops see it. Like my deputies say: shit happens. And then we come along and clean up the mess.

I guess maybe I do carry around that big roll of toilet paper, after all.

So, anyway, Helen had asked me to get another six-pack and some chips. She does like her Doritos. It was hot, especially for late October, and a few more beers sounded like a good idea. I worry about Helen drinking so much, but it's like the kid thing. We just don't talk about it anymore. What I usually do is drink right along with her, and then I don't feel so bad.

So I was headed up Canyon, fully intending to go to the Ralphs Supermarket on Arroyo, when I observed some suspicious activity at the old liquor store on the corner of Orchard and Canyon (if you want it in *cop-ese).*

Suspicious isn't the word for it. A couple of Mexican girls were coming out of the place. One was balancing a stack of cigarette cartons that was so high she couldn't see over it. The other had a couple of plastic sacks that looked to be filled with liquor bottles.

I pulled into the lot, tires squealing. The girl with the liquor bottles had pretty good instincts, because she dropped them and rabbited. The strong smell of tequila and rum hit me as I jumped out of the truck—a less sober-hearted man would have thought he'd died and gone to heaven. Me, I had other things on my mind.

The girl with the cigarettes hadn't gotten too far. She didn't want to give up her booty. Cartons were slipping and sliding and she looked like a drunken trapeze artist about to take the big dive, but she was holding tough.

Tackling her didn't seem like the best idea, but I sure didn't want to let her work up any steam. I'm not as fast as I used to be. So what I did was I grabbed for her hair, which was long enough to brush her ass when she wasn't running and it wasn't streaming out behind her. I got a good grip first try; her feet went out from under her, she shrieked like a starlet in a horror movie who's about to taste chainsaw, the smokes went flying every which way, and it was just damn lucky for me that she wasn't wearing a wig.

"It wasn't me!" she said, trying to fight. "I didn't do it! It was some guy wearing a mask!"

"Yeah, right. And you've got a receipt for these cigarettes in your back pocket. Sorry…got you red-handed, little miss."

I hustled her across the lot, stomping cigarette cartons as I went. That gave me a kick. God, I hate smokers. We went inside the store, and that's when I saw what she'd meant when she said she hadn't done anything.

The kid was no more than twenty, and—like the old saying goes—he'd never see twenty-one. He lay on the floor, a pool of dark blood around the hole in his head.

"We saw the guy who did it," the girl said, eager to please, *real* eager to get my fingers out of her hair. "He cleaned out the register. He was wearing a mask…"

Dead eyes stared up at me. My right boot toed the shore of a sea of blood. Already drying, going from red to a hard black on the yellow linoleum. Going down, the clerk had tripped over a stack of newspapers, and they were scattered everywhere. My face was on the front page of every paper, ten or twenty little faces, most of them splattered with blood.

"...a Halloween mask," she continued. "A pumpkin with a big black grin. We weren't with him. We pulled in after it was over, but we saw him leaving. I think he was driving an El Camino. It was silver, and it had those tires that have the chrome spokes. We were gonna call you before we left, honest. We figured the clerk was already dead, and that we'd just take what we wanted and—"

"Let it lay." I finished it for her, and she had the common decency to keep her mouth shut.

I just stood there for a minute, looking at the dead kid. It was like looking at myself thirty years ago. Like that poem about roads not taken. I almost envied him. Then I couldn't see him anymore—I saw myself at eighteen, so I looked away.

At the papers, at my smiling face.

At the headline: HERO RESCUES BABY FROM WELL.

Some hero. A grinning idiot with blood on his face.

The Mexican girl couldn't wait anymore. She'd run out of common decency and was starting to worry about herself again.

She opened her mouth.

I slapped her before she could say anything stupid. My fingers striking hard against her tattooed tears.

"The other girl got away," I said. "I'll bet she had the gun. Long black hair, about five-six, maybe a hundred pounds. Maybe a little more...it's hard to tell with those baggy jackets they wear. Anyway, she probably tossed the weapon. We'll beat the bushes on Orchard. That can wait until tomorrow, though."

Kat Gonzalez nodded, scribbling furiously. She was one of ten deputies who worked under me, and she was the best of the lot.

"I'm leaving this in your hands, Kat. I mean to tell you, I'm all in." I wanted to take a six-pack from the cooler, but I resisted the temptation. "I'm going home."

Kat stopped me with a hand on my shoulder. "Sheriff.... Hell, Dutch, I know what happened here when you were a kid. This must feel pretty weird. But don't let it eat at you. Don't—"

I waved her off before she could get started. "I know."

"If you need to talk—"

"Thanks." I said it with my back to her, and the only reason it came out okay was that I was already out the door.

I stomped a few more cigarette cartons getting to my truck, but it didn't make me feel any better. The night air was still heavy with the aroma of tequila and rum, only now it was mixed with other less appealing parking lot odors. Burnt motor oil. Dirt. Piss.

Even so, it didn't smell bad, and that didn't do me any good. Because it made me want something a hell of a lot stronger than beer.

I drove to Ralphs and bought the biggest bottle of tequila they had.

I was eighteen years old when I shot my first man.

Well, he wasn't a man, exactly. He was seventeen. And he was my brother.

Willie died on Halloween night in 1959. He was wearing a rubber skull mask that glowed in the dark, and "Endless Sleep" was playing on the radio when I shot him. He'd shown up at the store on the corner of Canyon and Orchard—it was a little mom-and-pop joint back then. With him was another boy, Johnny Halowenski, also wearing a mask.

A pumpkin face with a big black grin.

They showed up on that warm night in 1959 wanting money. The store had been robbed three times in the last two months, each time during my shift. The boss had said I'd lose my job if it happened again. I'd hidden my dad's .38 under the counter, and the two bandits didn't know about it.

Skullface asked for the money. I shot him instead. I didn't kill him, though. Not at first. He had enough spit left in him to come over the counter after me. I had to shoot him two more times before he dropped.

By then Pumpkinface had gotten away. I came out of the store just in time to see his Chevy burning rubber down Orchard, heading for the outskirts of town. There wasn't any question about who he was. No question at all. I got off a couple more shots, but none of them were lucky.

I went inside and peeled off the dead bandit's skull mask. I sat there stroking my brother's hair, hating myself, crying.

Then I got myself together and called the sheriff's office.

When the deputies arrived, I told them about Johnny Halowenski. I didn't know what else to do. They recognized the name. L.A. juvie had warned them about him. Johnny had steered clear of trouble since moving to our town, and the deputies had been willing to go along with that and give him a break.

But trouble had caught up with Johnny Halowenski in a big way.

I knew that, and I laid it on. My dad had been a deputy before he got too friendly with the whiskey bottle, and I knew it was important to get things right, to make sure that Halowenski wouldn't be able to get away with anything if the cops caught up to him.

I told the deputies that Halowenski was armed and dangerous.

I told the deputies that Halowenski took off his mask as he climbed into the Chevy, that there could be no mistake about his identity.

Everything I said ended up in the papers. There were headlines from Los Angeles to San Francisco about the Halloween murder/robbery at a liquor store near the border and the ensuing manhunt.

One paper mentioned that the suspect's nickname was Johnny Halloween. After that I never saw it any other way. Almost every year I'd see it a few times. In FBI wanted posters. In cheap magazines that ran stories about unsolved crimes. And, on Halloween, I could always count on it turning up in the local papers.

Johnny Halloween. I leaned back against my brother's granite tombstone and stared up at the night sky, trying to pick out the name in the bright stars above.

Drinking tequila, thinking how I'd never seen that name where I wanted to.

On a tombstone.

I knew he'd show up sooner or later, because we always met in the cemetery after the robberies.

Johnny came across the grass slow and easy, his pistol tucked under his belt, like the last thing in the world he wanted to do was startle me. I tossed him the bottle when he got near enough. "Let's drink it down to the worm," I said.

He didn't take a drink, though. He would have had to lift his mask, and he didn't seem to want to do that, either.

"Miss me?" he asked, laughing, and his laughter was bottled up inside the mask, like it couldn't quite find its way out of him.

"It's been a while," I said. "But not long enough to suit me."

He tossed me a thin bundle of bills. "Here's your cut. It's the usual third. I don't figure you've still got my dough from the last job. If I could collect interest on it, it might amount to something."

I didn't say anything to that. I didn't want to rise to the bait.

"Well, hell…it's good to see you too, Dutch. The old town hasn't changed all that much in thirty years. I went by my daddy's house, and damned if he isn't still driving that same old truck. Babyshit-brown Ford with tires just as bald as he is. Seventy-five years old and still drives like a bat out of hell, I'll bet. How about your daddy? He still alive?"

I pointed two graves over.

"Yeah, well…I bet you didn't shed too many tears. The way he used to beat hell out of you and Willie, I'm here to tell you. Man could have earned money, throwin' punches like those—"

That hit a nerve. "Just why are you here, Johnny?"

Again, the bottled-up laugh. "Johnny? Hell, that's a kid's name, Dutch. Nobody's called me that in twenty-five years. These days I go by Jack."

"Okay, Jack. I'll stick with the same question, though."

"Man, you're still one cold-hearted son of a bitch. And I thought you'd gone and mellowed. Become a humanitarian. Do you know that your picture made the Mexico City dailies? Sheriff rescues baby from well. That took some kind of big brass *cojones,* I bet."

My face had gone red, and I didn't like it. "There wasn't anything to it," I said. "I found the baby. I'm the sheriff. What was I supposed to do?"

We were both quiet for a moment.

"Look, Johnny—Jack—I'm tired. I don't mind telling you that the years have worn on me, and I don't have much patience anymore. Why don't you start by giving me your gun. I'm going to need it for evidence. I've already got one suspect in custody—nobody will ever connect what happened tonight to you. So you can figure you got your revenge, and you can tell me how much money you want, and we can get on with our lives."

"You know," he said, "I hadn't thought about you for years and years. And then I saw that picture in the paper, and damned if I wasn't surprised that you'd actually gone and become a cop. Man oh man, that idea took some getting used to. So I said to myself, *Jack, now you've just got to go see old Dutch before you die, don't you?*"

He knelt before me, his blue eyes floating in the black triangles of that orange mask. "See, I wanted to thank you," he said. "Going to Mexico was the best thing that ever happened to me. I made some money down there. Had a ball. They got lots of pretty boys down there, and I like 'em young and dark. Slim, too—you know, before all those frijoles and tortillas catch up to 'em. You never knew that about me, did you, Dutch? Your brother did, you know. I had a real hard-on for his young ass, but he only liked pussy. You remember how he liked his pussy? Man, how he used to talk about it. Non-fucking-stop! Truth be told, I think he maybe liked the talkin' better than the doin'. And *you* so shy and all. Now that was funny. You two takin' your squirts under the same skirt."

"You got a point in here somewhere, or are you just trying to piss me off?"

"Yeah. I got a point, Dutch."

Johnny Halloween took off the pumpkin mask, and suddenly I had the crazy idea that he was wearing Willie's skull mask beneath it. His blue eyes were the same and his wild grin was the same, but the rest of his face was stripped down, as if someone had sucked all the juice out of him.

"It's what you get when you play rough with pretty boys and don't bother to wear a raincoat," he said. "AIDS. The doctors say it ain't even bad yet. I don't want it to get bad, y'see."

I stared at him. I couldn't even blink.

He gave me the gun. "You ready to use it now?"

I shook my head. "I'm sorry," I said, and I was surprised to find that I really meant it.

"Let me help you out, Dutch." That wild grin welded on Death's own face. "See, there's a reason it took me so long to get to the cemetery tonight. I had to swing past your place and talk to Helen. Did a little trick-or-treating and got me some Snickers. Nothing more, nothing less. And when I'd had my fill, I told her everything."

There was nothing I could say....

"Now, I want you to do it right the first time, Dutch. Don't drag it out."

...so I obliged him.

It took two hours to get things done. First I heaved up as much tequila as I could. Then I drove ten miles into the desert and dumped Johnny Halloween's corpse. Next I headed back to the cemetery, got in Johnny's El Camino, and drove two miles north to a highway rest stop. There were four or five illegals standing around who looked like they had no place to go and no way to get there. I left the windows down and the keys in the ignition and I walked back to the cemetery, hoping for the best.

On the way home I swung down Orchard and tossed Johnny's pistol into some oleander bushes three houses up from the liquor store.

My house was quiet. The lights were out. That was fine with me. I found Helen in the kitchen and untied her. I left the tape over her mouth until I said my piece.

I didn't get through the whole thing, though. Toward the end I ran out of steam. I told her that Johnny and Willie and me had pulled the robberies because we hated being so damn poor. That it seemed easier to take the money than not to take it, with me being the clerk and such a good liar besides. I explained that the Halloween job was going to be my last. That I'd been saving those little scraps of money so we could elope, so our baby wouldn't have to come into the world a bastard.

It hurt me, saying that word. I never have liked it. Just saying it in front of Helen is what made me start to crack.

My voice trembled with rage and I couldn't control it anymore. "Johnny took me over to his house that day," I said. "All the time laughing through that wild grin. He had me peek in the window…and I saw Willie on top of you…and I saw you smiling…."

I slapped Helen then, just the way I'd slapped the Mexican girl at the liquor store, like she didn't mean anything to me at all.

"I was crazy." I clenched my fists, fighting for control. "You know how I get…. Everything happened too damn fast. They came to the store that night, and I was still boiling. I planned to kill them both and say I hadn't known it was them because of the masks, but it didn't work out that way. Sure, I shot Willie. But I had to shoot him three times before he died. I wanted to kill Johnny, too, but he got away. So I changed the story I'd planned. I hid Willie's skull mask, and I hid the gun and the money, and I said that Willie had been visiting me at the store when a lone bandit came in. That bandit was Johnny Halloween, and he'd done the shooting. And all the time that I was lying, I was praying that the cops wouldn't catch him."

I blew my nose and got control of myself. Helen's eyes were wide in the dark, and there was a welt on her cheek, and she wasn't moving. "I was young, Helen," I told her. "I didn't know what to do. It didn't seem right—getting married, bringing a baby into the world when I couldn't be sure that I was the father. I wanted everything to be just right, you know? It seemed like a good idea to use the money for an abortion instead of a wedding. I figured we'd just go down to Mexico, get things taken care of. I figured we'd have plenty of time for kids later on."

That's when I ran out of words. I took the tape off of Helen's mouth, but she didn't say anything. She just sat there.

I hadn't said so much to Helen in years.

I handed her the tequila bottle. There was a lot left in it.

Her hands shook as she took it. The clear, clean liquor swirled. The worm did a little dance. I turned away and quit the room, but not fast enough to miss the gentle slosh as she tipped back the bottle.

I knew that worm didn't stand a chance.

I don't know why I went out to the garage. I had to go somewhere, and I guess that's where a lot of men go when they want to be alone.

I shuffled some stuff around in my toolbox. Cleaned up the workbench. Changed the oil in the truck. Knowing that I should get rid of the pumpkin mask, but just puttering around instead.

All the time thinking. Questions spinning around in my head.

Wondering if Helen would talk.

Wondering if I'd really be able to pin the clerk's murder on the Mexican girls. Not only if the charges would stick, but if I had enough left in me to go through with it.

Wondering if my deputies would find Johnny's corpse, or his El Camino, or if he'd left any other surprises for me that I didn't know about.

They were the kind of questions that had been eating at me for thirty years, and I was full up with them.

My breaths were coming hard and fast. I leaned against the workbench, staring down at the pumpkin mask. Didn't even know I was crying until my tears fell on oily rubber.

It took me a while to settle down.

I got a .45 out of my tool chest. The silencer was in another drawer. I cleaned the gun, loaded it, and attached the silencer.

I stared at the door that led to the kitchen, and Helen. Those same old questions started spinning again. I closed my eyes and shut them out.

And suddenly I pictured Johnny Halloween down in Mexico, imagined all the fun he'd had over the years with his pretty boys and his money. Not my kind of fun, sure. But it must have been something.

I guess the other guy's life always seems easier. Sometimes I think even Willie's life was easier. I didn't want to start thinking that way with a gun in my hands.

I opened my eyes.

I unwrapped a Snickers bar, opened the garage door. The air held the sweet night like a sponge. The sky was going from black to purple, and soon it would be blue. The world smelled clean and the streets were empty. The chocolate tasted good.

I unscrewed the silencer. Put it and the gun in the glove compartment along with the three hundred and fifteen bucks Johnny Halloween had stolen from the liquor store.

Covered all of it with the pumpkin mask.
I felt a little better, a little safer, just knowing it was there.

SATAN'S ARMY

Tonight is his night! Halloween belongs to the Prince of Darkness! It's not a night for children, and it's certainly not a night for celebration. No, it's a night to be wary, a night to lock your doors and read your Bible. And I know that's exactly what you good folks would be doing if the stakes weren't so high, right here, right now.

"I want to say that I'm very proud that you've chosen to be here with me, standing shoulder to shoulder against those who stand with the enemy. And I mean that, for those who stand against us stand with Satan, and they are evil! Oh, they may *look* perfectly innocent—they may *look* like your neighbor or your librarian or your friendly grocery clerk—but we know 'em! We can sniff 'em out! Satan's army is marching, brothers and sisters, and we must stop it. Right here, right now!"

Reverend Woodbury spun from the podium and was off of the platform and into the waiting limousine before his followers could begin to applaud. His right-hand man, Brother Bishop, lagged a half step behind—a studied half step that allowed the crowd's riotous cheers to fill the limo before he slammed the bullet-proof door behind him.

Reverend Woodbury's strength of will was sometimes a fragile thing, and Brother Bishop wouldn't allow it to be tested tonight. "Listen to them," he said. "They love you, Woody. They really feel the Holy Spirit."

"I hope the rest of the evening goes so smoothly. Any more speeches? I don't mind saying that my voice has about had it."

"Let's see. You've hit the prayer rally down at the church on Virginia Street, the school board meeting, the demonstration over at that theatre that's showing *The Wizard of Oz*, and unless you want to hit that video store over on the Florida Street Mall—"

"No. I'd just say the same things I said about *Oz*, and then I'd have to listen to those TV reporters ask their asinine questions all over again. Lord, how those fools try to make it all seem so silly. They can't understand how a child's mind accepts evil. They think that a story about wizards and witches is just innocent fun and games. Why, that filthy tale is nothing but dark magic and murder. It glorifies the supernatural! I tell you Bishop, we've got to stop it! All of it!"

Brother Bishop patted his friend's knee. "We're going to stop it. Tonight will be the last Halloween this city will ever see. Now, don't you worry about that."

"Hand over the crowbar."

"You want it now? Ain't there an alarm, or—"

"This is a public library, not Fort Knox. Generally speaking, such institutions don't have elaborate surveillance systems."

"You mean there ain't an alarm, right?"

"Look, just give me the crowbar."

Vicky Taylor passed a bag of Hershey's Kisses over the grocery scanner, following it with a bag of Snickers, a package of Reese's Peanut Butter Cups, and two bags of 3 Musketeers.

"Marge, did you leave *anything* on aisle nine?" Vicky asked.

The town librarian smiled. "I just hope I haven't missed all the trick-or-treaters. That damn school board meeting ran into overtime, as usual. Our friend Woodbury went on a regular filibuster."

Vicky sighed. "I would have been there, but old man Myers put me on the night shift this week. He's been treating me like pond slime since I went to that city council meeting with you. In fact, I'm beginning to think that he's a member of the reverend's flock."

"Y'know, it's getting so you can't tell the good guys from the bad guys around here."

"That's the truth. How'd the meeting go, anyway?"

"Not good. The board agreed to pull *The Wizard of Oz* from the grammar school library."

"You're kidding!"

"Nope. They say they're going to keep one copy behind the desk to circulate to kids whose parents sign a consent form, but you know how long that'll last—I'll bet my ACLU card that one of the reverend's followers will have their little angel borrow the book and 'lose' it."

Money changed hands. "I guess they'll be coming after your copies next."

"Yeah. They won't get them so easily, though. Woodbury may have that sad excuse for a school librarian in his pocket, but he doesn't have me."

Vicky bagged the groceries. "I wish I could have been there. I've got three kids in that school. They've all read the *Oz* books, and they haven't sacrificed the family cat to the powers of darkness. Not yet, anyway."

"Who's taking care of the little darlings tonight?"

"First they're going trick-or-treating on their own. That's until nine. Then they're going to report to the Johnsons next door."

Marge cradled the grocery bag. "Ah, the pleasures of single parenthood. Look, I'll give the little angels lots of candy if they come my way. What costumes should I look for?"

Vicky winked. "I've got one Tin Woodman, one Cowardly Lion, and one Dorothy."

"Oh, you devil you," Marge said.

"Reverend Woodbury, do you really believe that the flying monkeys and talking apple trees in The Wizard of Oz *are agents of Satan?"*

"That kind of question trivializes our point of view. On the whole, this kind of fantasy ruins young minds. It takes our sons and daughters away from the Christian world, the real world. It endangers their innocent souls. Just like this Halloween holiday, just like that Dungeons & Dragons game, films of this kind cajole and tempt young people into accepting Satan."

"So, simply put, what you're saying is that The Wizard of Oz *leads to satanic worship?"*

"There you go again, putting words in my mouth. I'm saying that the Devil is strong in this country today, and getting stronger every second. Incidents of ritual abuse have been well documented. Sites of satanic worship are being discovered all the time—in public parks, in public buildings, right here in suburbia. But some people don't want us to see the reality of the situation. They'd have us believe that incidents of graveyard vandalism are just youthful hi-jinks, not ceremonies that pay tribute to—"

"We interrupt this interview with a report of a fire at the Florida Street Mall. It appears that the blaze began at Pandora's Box, a video store that specializes in fantasy and horror films. The business closed early this evening after a demonstration by members of Reverend Woodbury's Christcorps degenerated into a fistfight between customers and demonstrators, and the fire began shortly after local police—"

"Dad, turn off that television and help me wash these apples."

"Glad to, Mother. Just the same old stuff, anyhow."

"I said wash 'em, don't bruise 'em."

"Well, crikey, this water's cold. Bound to lose my grip on one or two, with my arthritis."

"Lord, I hate fires. My favorite yarn shop is two doors down from that video place, and I sure hope it doesn't burn."

"Oh, I don't know, Mother. Maybe you'll get to go to a fire sale."

"That's not funny, Dad."

"S'pose you're right. Y'know, this town used to be a pretty nice place to live."

"Maybe it will be again."

"Yep…Good apples this year. Big. Green…"

"So, Miss Vicky Taylor, I imagine that your children are out doing the Devil's business tonight."

"Look, Alice, I'm just here to total your groceries. Let's leave it at that."

"Not a chance! If you think I'm going to buy my family's food from one of Lucifer's harlots, you've got another thing coming. I just won't, that's all! You can spend the rest of your evening putting these things back on the shelves, and you can tell your boss that I'll be shopping elsewhere until you're fired! And one more thing: you keep your little imps away from my door, *Miss* Vicky Taylor, or I'll swat them with my Bible and send them straight to hell!"

The woman stalked off. Vicky stared at the full cart of groceries. Myers would be furious when he heard about the Christcorps' latest form of protest, and the stock clerks wouldn't be pleased about it, either. Especially if such dramatics got to be a regular event.

Vicky pushed the cart aside. She imagined Alice Wentworth sitting in her car, telling her prayer pals how well her stunt had worked.

Our little reverend's just full of tricks, isn't he? Vicky thought as she returned to the register.

A man was waiting for her. Judging from the way he was carrying on, Vicky guessed that he'd seen the entire incident.

She grinned. The man was wearing a Scarecrow costume complete with a burlap mask. He had one finger pointed at his forehead, and he said in a rough voice, "If I only had a brain. Am I right?"

Vicky laughed and rang up the man's purchases.

Eight T-bone steaks. Twelve candles. A coil of rope. A pumpkin. A can of lighter fluid.

The Scarecrow paid her. She bagged the items.

"Keep the faith," he said, and then he wobbled out the door, as crazy-legged as Ray Bolger ever was.

"I never seen so many books."

"Here we are. 133.4. Bag 'em."

"Right away. Boy, who would have ever thought that people would write so much about this kind of stuff?"

"It sure does make the head spin, doesn't it? C'mon, get busy...Okay. That's enough. I'll carry these out to the car. You take the flashlight and go find that book the boss wanted."

"Sure. What's the number on it?"

"It's fiction, not nonfiction."

"Yeah. Right. But what's the number on it?"

"Apples are all clean, Mother."

"Good job, Dad. Now comes the hard part."

"Gee whiz. Ain't seen one of these since you gave me the safety razor last Christmas."

"That was two Christmases ago, Dad. Now, mind you don't cut yourself."

Beautiful view from up here, the Scarecrow thought. *Stars above and city below.*

His assistants had already planted the fence posts. The Scarecrow peeled plastic wrap and Styrofoam away from the T-bones. He circled the posts, squeezing blood from the meat. Then he crisscrossed the circle, blood dribbling between his gloved fingers as he formed the sign of the pentagram.

The Scarecrow's assistants pulled lengths of kindling from the bed of the rented pickup truck. While the masked man placed candles around the circle, they piled the wood around the posts.

"Not too much just yet." The Scarecrow's words puffed the burlap mask away from his face. "Remember, we've got to tie 'em to the posts first, and you might get yourself a nasty splinter scrambling around knee-deep in tinder."

The men laughed. One moved to light a cigarette.

"I didn't say that you should quit working." The Scarecrow pointed at the truck. "One of you can carve the pumpkin. And someone better make sure that cat hasn't scratched its way out of that burlap sack."

Marge caught the phone on the third ring. "Is this Marge King, the librarian?"

"Yes. That's me."

"Got your nose in a big thick book, bitch? Or do you got a big thick book jammed up your filthy cunt while you dream about Satan's big black cock? Bet you like that, huh? Bet you get all juicy dreaming about—"

The librarian slammed down the receiver. Stared at the phone. Waited for it to ring again.

No. Not tonight. She'd heard more than enough for one night.

The doorbell rang, and she nearly jumped out of her skin.

Hating the fear that made her fingers shake, Marge King unplugged the phone.

She answered the door, a basket of candy cradled under one arm.

No one was there.

"Well, Henry, thanks for letting me use your phone."

"Don't mention it."

"Say, mind if I help myself to an apple?"

"Well, not *those* apples."

"Oh yeah. Silly me."

"Here you go. Saved this one for you special."

"Thanks, Henry. My, but you grow the best...Big and green."

"Whoa, now. There's that danged doorbell again...and here's the little woman. Mother, take a look at your favorite Brother!"

"Why, I'll be. I just wouldn't know you, Brother Bishop!"

"Sally, tonight I wouldn't even know myself."

The Tin Woodman, the Cowardly Lion, and Dorothy stood at the door.

"What d'ya think we'll get?"

"Last year they had pears and oranges."

"Then why'd we save this house for last?"

"Don't be stupid, sis."

The door opened and the old man smiled down at them. "Well, hello kids! C'mon in, I've got someone here I want you to meet…a Munchkin, *di*-rect from Oz!"

"Oh boy," Dorothy whispered. "I don't think I can *stand* the excitement."

The Tin Woodman and the Cowardly Lion giggled.

A tall man wearing a Munchkin costume danced across the room.

"You're awfully big for a Munchkin," Dorothy said.

"Ho ho, little miss! If you think *I'm* big, just wait till you meet the Scarecrow!"

"It's Tiger!" Dorothy shouted as she ran up the hill. "My little kitty's here!"

"Of course he is," the Scarecrow said, stroking the animal. "What's Dorothy without her Toto?"

The library burglars grabbed Dorothy and the Cowardly Lion. The big Munchkin grabbed the Tin Woodman's Boy Scout ax, threw it into the bushes, and dragged the Tin Woodman up the hill. The boy's costume rattled as if something had broken deep inside him.

Kicking, screaming, the three children were wrestled into the circle and tied to the fence posts. Frightened by their protests, the cat sprang from the Scarecrow's arms.

Dorothy squirmed against her bonds. "Run, Tiger, run!"

The men piled high the tinder.

Squirted it with lighter fluid.

Sweat stung the Scarecrow's cheeks. He scratched at his burlap mask, but that only made the itch worse.

"I know why you're doing this," Dorothy said.

The Scarecrow asked the library burglars for the book with the Yellow Brick Road on its cover. He squirted the worn pages with lighter fluid and hefted the book with one gloved hand.

"Light it up," he said.

"You mean they never showed up?"

"Look, Vicky, kids will be kids. Maybe they're still out running around the neighborhood. After all, it's Halloween—"

"And they didn't call?"

"Well, they didn't call me. How about it, Mother? Did they phone you?"

"No, Dad. They sure didn't."

Vicky sighed. "Henry...Sally...I'm sorry to put you out. You've both been such good neighbors. When they show up, will you send them straight home?"

"Sure thing. G'night, Vicky."

The door closed. Vicky turned away from the Johnson's house, toward her empty, silent home.

She stared at the sky. A green haze lingered over the hills beyond town, hanging just below the purple darkness. A trick of reflected city lights, she imagined.

Vicky smiled. A green glow, like the lights of Oz.

Suddenly, a patch of red erupted amid the green.

Vicky watched, transfixed, And then realization and fear kicked in at the same instant, and she ran for the telephone.

The bullet-proof limo rolled out of town.

"Bishop, if everyone believes it, then can it be a lie?"

"No, not a lie. A parable, spread by the media with photos and videotape and physical documentation. A creative truth, if you will."

"Guerilla theatre—that's what the bleeding hearts call it."

"Call it what you like, Woody."

"But don't call it murder?"

"Sometimes these things are necessary. Sometimes, as with David and Goliath, it's a simple matter of them or us."

"I know, Bishop. I know. But the way that Satan hides in the most innocent places, and the things we have to do to fight him…well, sometimes it disturbs me."

"Of course it does. You wouldn't be one of God's creatures if it didn't. But look at it this way: we've destroyed the evil in this town. Maybe in the entire state. After tonight, it won't rear its ugly head in these parts ever again. Good folks won't allow that. Believe me, Woody, they won't forget what happened here anytime soon. They'll be on guard from this day forward, and without our little drama, that would never have happened."

"Still, the look in that little girl's eyes…. The way she stared at me, without fear, as if she could see through my mask, as if she possessed some righteous power—"

Brother Bishop gripped the reverend's arm. "That was the Evil One, Woody. Don't you see? That was Lucifer himself, tempting you."

The reverend nodded. He leaned back, closed his eyes, and massaged his cheeks, which were dotted with swollen red blotches.

"Bishop," he said, "I don't want to smell or see or feel burlap…ever again."

THE MAN WHO KILLED HALLOWEEN

For kids growing up in the sixties, Halloween was the best of holidays. Costumed boys and girls hit the streets in packs. As night fell entire neighborhoods were transformed into creepshow carnivals.

Judging by today's Spookshow Superstore standards, Halloween wasn't anywhere near wild. In suburban America circa 1968, you'd be hard pressed to find a house with a full-on animatronic display in the front yard featuring giant wriggling arachnids, the way you can today. "Professional" haunted houses with chainsaw-wielding actors and soon-to-be bisected actresses were unknown as well, and you sure weren't going to see any adult stepping out in full *Rocky Horror* regalia. Stuff like that just didn't exist. In those days Halloween meant monsters, and America served up the old cinematic standards who'd been creeping around since the thirties: Frankenstein, Dracula, the Wolf Man and the Mummy.

So '68 wasn't exactly the Halloween that dripped blood. It wasn't plug-in, and it wasn't sexy. What it was was a hand-carved pumpkin on the porch, a big bowl of candy behind the front door, and a TV tuned to an old Universal Studios chiller. Barring the occasional old lady who'd dress up as a witch to scare any kiddies who dared to ring her doorbell, few adults wore costumes, or had parties, or did much more than dole out candy.

In those days, Halloween was for kids. Those who'd reached double digits age-wise mostly made their own costumes, while the under-ten population dressed in outfits purchased at the local five-and-dime. Kids transformed themselves into cut-rate fairy princesses and witches, hippies and soldiers, Tarzan of the Apes and George of the Jungle, and all four Beatles. They made the rounds of the neighborhood, collecting their booty in pillowcases or grocery bags, ringing as many doorbells as possible before the clock ticked its way toward the inexorable parental curfew.

If you started early and moved fast, you could get enough candy to last a month. And if you planned ahead and hit the right houses early enough, you could score stuff that was better than candy—some folks actually gave out homemade treats like popcorn balls and candy apples, and recipients didn't worry that they'd end up choking on razor blades secreted in same. I mean, you got this stuff from your *neighbors*. You knew where they *lived*.

That's the way it was in the town where I grew up. Vallejo, California, was home to Mare Island Naval Shipyard. The Yard brought lots of people to town during World War II, and many of them stayed once the war was over. By the time the sixties rolled around, Mare Island was turning out nuclear submarines and business was booming. Economically more blue collar than white, Vallejo was the kind of place where most of the dads worked at the shipyard and most of the moms stayed home to tend the kids.

That last score was a little different in my family. Both my parents worked. Mom was a railroad clerk, and Dad was a truck driver. The old man, in particular, loved Halloween, and in '68 he went all out. That year he pulled up in the driveway after work, his pickup loaded with big cardboard boxes. It didn't take me long to figure out that they were cases of Cracker Jack. I'm not talking special treat-size Cracker Jack, either. These were the real deal. Each case was filled with full-size boxes of caramel corn, nuts, and (as the old advertisement promised), a prize in every pack.

We stacked the cases in the entry hall. Arriving home from work, my mom took one look at all those boxes and nearly had a stroke—she was sure the old man had blown a week's grocery money on trick-or-treat swag, but Dad had the only answer guaranteed to save his hide all ready to go. When Mom asked where he'd gotten all that Cracker Jack, he gave her his best Jimmy Hoffa Teamster smile and said: "Don't worry, Ev. It fell off a truck."

In all the years my dad drove trucks for a living, that load of Cracker Jack was the most memorable thing that ever "fell off" one of them. Around the neighborhood, word about the good stuff to be had at the Partridge's house spread fast. We lived on a hill so steep that you had to cut switchbacks to climb it on a bicycle, but that didn't matter. Our doorbell didn't stop ringing all night. By the time I got home from my own trick-or-treating expedition, we were cleaned out. Every box of Cracker Jack was gone, and the old man was raiding my piggy bank for change to give the kids who'd climbed our hill expecting a box.

That was the Halloween I'll always remember, and—just like the Cracker Jack—I was sorry to see it go. The next day we tossed out our candle-scorched jack-o'-lantern, flattened the big cardboard boxes that had held the Cracker Jack and tossed them, too. I started marking time until the next big holiday—Christmas—and when Christmas had come and gone I waited as the clock slowly spun toward summer vacation, and three fast months after that I was back in school counting the days until Halloween night, 1969.

But by the time that night arrived, everything had changed in my hometown. There weren't many kids ringing doorbells that year. There weren't many kids on the streets at all. Because someone was out there that Halloween, someone scarier than all the bogeymen I'd ever seen on television or at the movies, someone *pit-of-the-stomach-frightening* enough to keep me inside on my favorite night of the year.

That someone was a real monster.

He was a serial killer.

He called himself the Zodiac.

On December 20, 1968, two teenagers went out on a first date. David Faraday told Betty Lou Jensen's parents that they were going to a Christmas carol concert, and maybe to a party afterwards.

David and Betty Lou were from opposite sides of town. They attended different schools, but that didn't really matter. Most kids in Vallejo went to one of two public high schools—Vallejo High or James J. Hogan—and while the schools enjoyed a cross-town rivalry, students from both institutions shared the same drive-in's, movie theaters, and burger joints. It was only natural that some of them would date.

David and Betty Lou decided to skip the Christmas concert and stopped for a Coke at Mr. Ed's, a hangout located at one end of the local strip. After that they drove down Springs

Road, maybe passing friends who were out cruising with their car radios tuned to KFRC or KYA, the local top 40 stations.

The pair left the strip and turned onto Columbus Parkway. Making that turn, David and Betty Lou would have known that they were leaving any possibility of going to a party behind. And following Columbus to Lake Herman Road would have meant only one thing to a couple kids from Vallejo—that they were heading toward the local lovers' lane.

If you were a teenager looking for privacy, Lake Herman Road was one of the places you'd find it. It wasn't the only place—there was the parking lot at Blue Rock Springs, and the overlook near the Carquinez Straits where young couples parked to watch "the submarine races," and there was Benicia State Park, an inlet along the straits where frogs made music in the cattails while crickets sang on the dry hillsides on summer nights—but Lake Herman Road was the spot David and Betty Lou chose that night. A two-lane country road that snaked through rolling hills and ranch land, the twisting ribbon of asphalt cut away from Vallejo and meandered toward the outskirts of neighboring Benicia. There were few lights out there, and fewer people. Mostly there were cattle, sheep, and Lake Herman itself—a quiet, lonely spot that was usually deserted by sunset.

David knew where to go. He pulled off the blacktop, tires crunching over gravel, and parked near a chainlink fence that bordered the Lake Herman pumping station. From that spot he'd be able to watch Lake Herman Road for cops. Officers often swung through the area on nightly patrol—the place David had parked was a favorite of underage drinkers and dope-smokers, as well as lovers.

It was a dark night. Rolling hills behind the couple cut off the lights from town. Few cars passed by as the next hour ticked off. But one of those cars stopped, parking a short distance from David's '61 Rambler.

After some time, a man got out of that car and walked toward the Rambler. No one can say for certain what happened in the next few minutes. But when those minutes had passed, David Faraday lay dying on the ground. He'd been shot in the head, point blank, with a .22-caliber pistol.

Betty Lou Jensen lay dead less than thirty feet away.

She'd taken five bullets in her back.

She was running toward Vallejo when she died.

But she never made it out of that gravel lot.

She never even made it as far as Lake Herman Road.

The murders hit the town hard. For a few days, people talked of little else. The police interviewed a pair of hunters who'd noticed David's Rambler parked off Lake Herman Road, but they hadn't seen the killer. Perhaps more significantly, a couple in a sports car who'd parked not far from David and Betty Lou about an hour and a half before the murders came forward with a story about a driver who'd slowed to a crawl as he passed them, then quickly reversed course and tailed them to the Benicia cutoff when they grew frightened and drove off.

For my part, seeing the story plastered across the front page of the local newspaper was like seeing a nightmare come to life. The Faraday/Jensen killings had all the trappings of tales I'd heard from older kids on hot summer nights: *the deserted road...two teenagers alone in a parked car...a hulking stranger approaching in the dark....* The familiarity of the scenario gave me a strangely prescient fright. It seemed I knew this story all too well, and this story, after all, was *real.* I could almost see it happening, and that scared me most of all. I saw the killer in my mind's eye the same way I saw the phantom hitchhikers in the stories told by my older brother and his friends. To tell the truth, if the couple in the sports car who escaped the phantom tailgater had reported that they'd found a hook-hand dangling from their car door when they hit the streets of Benicia, I wouldn't have been surprised. For me, the killings on Lake Herman Road were like an urban legend come to life.

But the story didn't last. It couldn't. The police didn't have any suspects. There were few leads. By all accounts, David Faraday and Betty Lou Jensen were a couple of good kids. The cold hard truth of it seemed to be that they'd died for one reason—they were in the wrong place at the wrong time.

Christmas came and went. The new year rang in on its heels.

More than half a year passed before the Zodiac marked another holiday with murder.

In June of '69 I finished off the fifth grade at Pennycook Elementary School, and I didn't even think about getting ready for the sixth. The summer stretched before me, three months that might include just about anything.

One thing that wasn't on my list was a bike ride on Lake Herman Road. The lake had been a favorite destination during previous summers, but I didn't know anyone who wanted to head out there after David and Betty Lou made their one-way trip in December. Not even on a brightly lit summer afternoon.

There were other places to go, though, places that wouldn't conjure up images of awful winter nights. Oddly enough, many of the daytime destinations enjoyed by younger kids doubled as lovers' lanes at night. Benicia State Park was a personal favorite of mine. So was Blue Rock Springs, a city park that bordered the local golf course. Nestled in a fragrant eucalyptus grove, Blue Rock was a place straight out of a fairy tale or an old Robin Hood movie. The trees were tall and dark, growing close together, and it was always cool in their shadows, even on the hottest days. A duck pond waited a stone's throw from the parking lot, and there were plenty of picnic tables where you could stretch out on your back, sip from a cold bottle of Coke, and stare up at the passing clouds in the summer sky.

From one of those picnic tables, you could easily see the golf course parking lot where the Lake Herman Road killer made his next strike. The date was July 4, 1969. Again, the killer struck on a holiday, and again he struck late at night. Again, he chose a couple parked alone in a remote area (the golf course parking lot at Blue Rock Springs was little more than two miles from the site of the Faraday/Jensen murders). Again, he used a gun, killing waitress Darlene Ferin and seriously wounding Mike Mageau as they sat in Darlene's '63 Corvair. And again, he escaped on a dark two-lane road, disappearing into the night.

A few weeks after the crime, the killer wrote letters to three Bay Area newspapers (including the *Vallejo Times-Herald*) in which he claimed responsibility for the murders. These letters included details of the crimes that only the killer and the police would know, and ciphers which the writer promised would reveal his identity. Each letter ended with a threat—if the ciphers weren't published, the writer promised to "go on a kill ram-Page Fry. Night. I will cruse around all weekend killing lone people in the night then move on to kill again, until I end up with a dozen people over the weekend."

All three ciphers were published, along with some text from the letters.

The killer wasn't satisfied, however.

A few days later, he mailed another letter to the *Vallejo Times-Herald.*

This time, he did reveal his identity.

The letter began:

Dear Editor

This is the Zodiac speaking….

Now the killer had a name, though he still didn't have a face.

The Zodiac was a shadow, albeit a deadly one, and that meant he might be almost anyone.

Someone we knew…or someone we only *thought* we knew.

Someone who could fool us.

Whatever the case, most people in town were sure that the Zodiac walked among us. The killer seemed to know Vallejo a little too well. The argument went this way—an outsider couldn't come into town and target two lovers' lanes so easily. A stranger wouldn't know his way around the way this guy did. Jesus, the killer was so sure of himself that he actually called the Vallejo P. D. from a pay phone in front of the Sheriff's Office after he'd killed Darlene Ferin. And he sent that last letter to the *Vallejo Times-Herald.* He didn't even bother to send it to the San Francisco papers. No one outside of Vallejo reads the *Times-Herald.* The Zodiac knows that, and he knows that *we* know that. That's what gets him off. He wants us to know he's *right here.*

Whether he was or whether he wasn't, my neighbors could feel him, could almost see him out of the corners of their eyes when the shadows grew long and darkness fell. Some odd geometry put nearly everyone I knew in proximity to one of the Zodiac's victims. My future sister-in-law lived just down the street from David Faraday's house. My brother Larry used to eat breakfast at Terry's, the restaurant where Darlene Ferin worked. Larry was a railroad switchman, worked lots of weird shifts, and came into the coffee shop at all hours. He thought he'd seen a white car around there, and a lone guy driving it. Nothing unusual about that, really. There were lots of white cars on the road, but word around town was that the Zodiac drove a white car, and that maybe he picked out Darlene Ferin as a victim because he knew her from Terry's.

Rumors swirled around for years in the wake left by the Zodiac's crimes, little bits and pieces of trivia that seemed to add up to something. I remember hearing a story about Mike Mageau, who survived multiple gunshot wounds at Blue Rock Springs. When police found him after the Zodiac's attack, it was said that Mageau was wearing three pairs of pants, a T-shirt, a long-sleeved shirt, and several sweaters…all on a hot summer night.

Everyone had a different explanation for the extra clothes. Some said Mageau was expecting a fight with someone—maybe a drug-dealing biker—who'd have a club or a chain, and that the clothes were padding that would allow him to stand up to punishment. Others said that he'd gone to Blue Rock Springs expecting to find a wild Fourth of July party. Young people sometimes had "firecracker wars" in remote spots around Vallejo during the Independence Day holiday, and the extra clothes would have been protection against any fireworks that would have been tossed Mageau's way. [4]

---

4 Years later, in *Zodiac*, the definitive exploration of the case, author Robert Graysmith revealed Mageau's own bizarre explanation for the extra clothes. Mageau said that he was self-conscious about being skinny and wore all those layers to "look huskier."

But in 1969, in the middle of it, we weren't concerned with mysterious little details like Mike Mageau's wardrobe. We were worried about a man with a gun. That summer, my friends and I spent many afternoons talking about the killer, wondering who he might be, devising traps that the police might use to catch him.

One friend—I'll call him Tim Alcott here—started a scrapbook of newspaper clippings about the Zodiac. Tim was a kid who had a bookcase full of Hardy Boys Mysteries. I think he figured that he could crack the case if he could just put together the clues in the right way, the way Frank and Joe Hardy would.

Before the arrival of the Zodiac's second letter, Tim was also convinced he could crack the three-part cipher the killer had mailed to Bay Area newspapers. One afternoon Tim took a bus down to the library, looking for some books on codes and crytography. He went to the card catalog and jotted down a few Dewey decimal numbers. Eager to get the books, he hurried to the stacks.

The library was cavernous, concrete, a disaster of sixties architecture bathed in dim florescent light. There were more shadows in the stacks than you were apt to find in that eucalyptus grove at Blue Rock Springs. Still, Tim went hunting for his books. He wanted to crack that cipher. He followed the Dewey numbers to 652.8, the section on codes and code-breaking.

Only problem was that the books weren't there.

Every book on the subject was already checked out.

Tim swallowed hard.

He thought he knew who had them.

My friend Tim didn't crack the Zodiac's cipher, but a Salinas high school teacher and his wife did:

**I LIKE KILLING PEOPLE
BECAUSE IT IS SO MUCH
FUN IT IS MORE FUN THAN
KILLING WILD GAME IN
THE FORREST BECAUSE
MAN IS THE MOST DANGEROUE
ANAMAL OF ALL TO KILL
SOMETHING GIVES ME THE
MOST THRILLING EXPERENCE
IT IS EVEN BETTER THAN GETTING
YOUR ROCKS OFF WITH A GIRL
THE BEST PART OF IT IS THAE
WHEN I DIE I WILL BE REBORN
IN PARADICE AND THEI HAVE
KILLED WILL BECOME MY SLAVES
I WILL NOT GIVE YOU MY NAME
BECAUSE YOU WILL TRY TO SLOI
DOWN OR ATOP MY COLLECTIOG OF
SLAVES FOR THE AFTERLIFE
EBEORIETEMETHHPITI**

The last line was thought to be an anagram for the killer's real name. My friends and I played around with it, trying out the names of adults we knew and didn't much like, but none of them fit. That didn't surprise me, but the message itself did. It sent a chill up my spine, because somehow it seemed...well, *familiar*. The part about man being *the most dangerous animal* reminded me of movies and television shows I'd seen where characters had uttered similar lines. And the part about collecting souls, well...that could have come from a dozen monster movies, the kind of movies I loved.

I reminded myself that this wasn't a movie.

Someone all-too-real had written the Zodiac cipher.

Someone sick enough to believe what he was writing.

I wasn't the only one who felt that way. My dad shook his head when he read the killer's decoded message. "The guy's a nut," he said. "You watch—he'll make a mistake, and they'll get him for sure."

But they didn't. The Zodiac struck again at the end of September. This time, the scene of the crime was Lake Berryessa, a man-made lake north of Vallejo where locals enjoyed fishing and picnicking.

The Zodiac targeted two college students, Cecelia Ann Shepard and Bryan Hartnell, who were relaxing on a blanket near the water's edge. The killer approached them with a drawn gun. He took their car keys and spoke to them. Hartnell tried to keep the man talking in hopes that the conversation might give him a chance to gain the upper hand. He began to think the whole thing was a simple robbery, only realizing how serious things were when the stranger decided to hogtie both his captives. Finally, the Zodiac attacked with a knife, killing Cecelia Ann and seriously wounding Hartnell.

Hartnell had noticed a lot about the killer. Recovering in the hospital, he described the Zodiac to the police—the man's manner, his voice, his size. One thing he couldn't describe was the Zodiac's face. The killer had worn a hood. It was black, squared off over the man's head like some strange executioner's mask, with a hanging bib that covered the killer's chest and bore the stitched "gunsight" insignia the Zodiac used in his letters.

Some people commented that the hood was almost like a Halloween costume.

A flip of the calendar page, and October came. But it wasn't the kind of October I'd enjoyed before, because Vallejo had become a different town.

People were extremely cautious. My dad insisted that my mom stop working her once-a-week night shift at the remote railroad depot on Highway 29, the road taken by anyone traveling between Vallejo and Lake Berryessa. Business slacked off at both of Vallejo's drive-in movie theaters. The burger joints on Springs Road were deserted after dark. And no one was cruising the strip.

With the whole town seemingly on alert, the Zodiac surprised everyone by taking his next victim in the heart of San Francisco. He killed a cab driver, Paul Lee Stine, and followed up the crime with another taunting letter to the *San Francisco Chronicle* that contained a piece of Stine's blood-stained shirt and a new threat:

> **School children make nice targets, I think I shall wipe out a school bus some morning. Just shoot out the front tire & then pick off the kiddies as they come bouncing out.**[5]

The threat was taken seriously. Armed police shadowed school buses in Napa. My friends and I were in the habit of walking to school or riding our bikes, but many parents thought that was too risky. Some started driving their kids to school,

5 A few years later, this threat provided the climax for Clint Eastwood's *Dirty Harry*, a film that featured a San Francisco cop tracking a serial killer obviously inspired by the Zodiac. Eastwood's nemesis, not-so-subtly, was called "Scorpio."

dropping them off, waiting and watching until they were safely in the classroom. Every day that passed increased the tension just a little bit, because everyone expected that there were more horrors to come.

The Zodiac's murders were coming closer together now.

So were his letters.

It seemed the killer was gearing up for something big.

On Wednesday, October 22nd, I got up early and started to get ready for school. The television was on downstairs, tuned to a call-in show featuring an affable host named Jim Dunbar. His guest was Melvin Belli, a San Francisco lawyer who had a reputation as a publicity hound.[6] Belli had been summoned to the show by a caller who'd phoned the Oakland police the night before. The caller identified himself as the Zodiac killer and promised to phone the show if Belli or fellow barrister F. Lee Bailey appeared.

Belli and Dunbar talked. And then the phone started to ring. The brief conversations with the caller on the other end were urgent, intense—the stranger speaking of his fear of the gas chamber and the headaches that tortured him, Belli urging the man to turn himself in. The caller hung up repeatedly, and then called back just as fast.

Remember, this was 1969, a long time before tabloid television. No one had ever seen anything like this. By the time the show was over, Belli had arranged to meet the caller that afternoon. Of course, the meeting never occurred, but that didn't matter. The seeds had been sown. When people arrived at work or school that day, they found that everyone was talking about the Dunbar show and the caller who claimed to be the Zodiac killer.

Later, the calls were traced to a psychiatric patient from Napa State Hospital, but no one knew that on October 22nd. The

6 Belli actually appeared as a villain on an episode of the original *Star Trek*.

caller's identity really didn't matter, anyway. What mattered was that anyone who heard the calls was rattled. The end result was the same—the fear meter had increased another notch.

And Halloween was right around the corner.

Each year on Halloween day at Pennycook Elementary School, students wore costumes to class. Even the teachers dressed up, and that was always fun for the kids. A sixth grade teacher showed up one year in full-on Batman regalia, looking more like the caped crusader than Adam West ever did. Even the dour old-maid types got into the act. I remember one rather large teacher who was a dead ringer for Ma Kettle (but without the sense of humor). This woman wore the same "costume" every year, consisting of nothing more than a child's plastic Cinderella mask. Looking back on it now, that mask makes me think that my fourth grade teacher was just a little sweeter than I ever might have guessed.

Each teacher hosted a little party for his or her class, and then the entire school paraded around the block, circling the playground while passing drivers honked their horns and waved. After that, students returned to their classrooms and waited for the final bell to ring, at which point they'd get down to the business of readying themselves for a long night of trick-or-treating.

None of that happened in 1969, of course. Sure, my friends and I wore costumes to school that day, but our celebration was confined to the classroom. The principal believed that a parade around the schoolyard might be just the thing the Zodiac was waiting for, and he decided not to tempt the killer.[7]

---

7 Ironically, the chief Zodiac suspect fingered by Robert Graysmith (and many others) was at the time employed as a janitor at another Vallejo elementary school, a school I'd attended just a few years before.

At home, as night fell, the mood wasn't any different. The few kids who were allowed out were restricted to a couple of neighborhood blocks where they were sure to know everyone. Most of my friends spent the night in front of the television, eating the few pieces of candy they'd managed to score, watching whatever monster was handy on television...and, most of all, remembering how wonderful Halloween had been just a year before.

We all knew who'd killed the day for us. We even knew what he looked like, because we'd finally gotten a glimpse under the Zodiac's executioner hood. After murdering the cabby in San Francisco, the killer had been spotted by a group of teenagers. A police artist made a drawing based on their description, and it was plastered over every front page in California.

Judging by the drawing, the Zodiac killer was not at all remarkable. He was a white man with short hair, thin lips, and a wrinkled brow. He wore horn-rimmed glasses over slitted, squinting eyes that bore a severe cast.

To me, the Zodiac's face seemed strangely unreal. Though not as obvious as a squared-off executioner's hood, it reminded me of another mask. The killer's severe eyes seemed to be staring at me through molded plastic slits, and I couldn't imagine his thin lips ever forming a smile. Seeing that face in the newspaper or on the wall at the post office, I was convinced that there was something missing from it, something as essential as a mouth or a nose though not as evident, but I could never decide what that missing thing was.

Paul Lee Stine, the San Francisco cab driver, was the Zodiac's last documented victim. The killer continued to send letters to Bay Area newspapers off and on through the mid-seventies, but he stopped naming his victims, saying that:

> **I have grown rather angry with the police for their telling lies about me. So I shall change the way the collecting of slaves. I shall no longer announce to anyone. when I comitt my murders, they shall look like routine robberies, killings of anger, & a few fake accidents, etc. The police shall never catch me, because I have been too clever for them.**

Perhaps he was too clever. Perhaps he did go on killing. No one can say for sure. As for the man himself: in one of his last his last authenticated letters (written in 1974), the Zodiac claimed to have murdered thirty-seven victims.

One thing's for certain—the killer was never apprehended. What really happened to him is anyone's guess. Some say that as the Zodiac grew older, his need to kill lessened. Some say illness incapacitated him. Some say he simply died, or was incarcerated for crimes other than murder, or was committed to a mental institution. Others insist he's still out there, waiting, perhaps, to strike again.

More than forty years after the murders on Lake Herman Road, Vallejo is a different place. The shipyard closed a long time ago, and the city never really recovered from the blow. The town is still home to retired people who remember the old days, and more than a few young people looking for an affordable place to live in the tight Bay Area housing market have joined them in setting down roots.

There are young families in town, too. Just like in the old days, most of the parents are blue collar workers. They raise their kids, send them to the same high schools that David Faraday and Betty Lou Jensen once attended. On October 31st, a lot of those kids go trick-or-treating, but the turnout isn't what it once was. Most households get by with one or two bags of candy. My mom, who still lives in the same house where I grew up, is lucky if twenty kids climb the hill and ring her doorbell. Even if she had cases of Cracker Jack stacked in the hallway, it wouldn't make a difference. The kids just don't come out the way they used to.

Some things in town haven't changed, though. Lake Herman Road is one of them. It was a lonely stretch of notmuch when the Faraday/Jensen murders were committed, and it was no different by the time I hit high school in the mid-seventies, when my friends and I would pack ourselves into a car on summer nights and drive out to the spot where two teenagers died in 1969, telling stories about the Zodiac, sharing the rumors we'd heard over the years, driving down that dark lonely stretch of blacktop...going slower...and slower...until we hit that one curve in the road and the tires crunched over gravel, and the guy behind the wheel stopped the car cold and killed the headlights, and we sat there in the dark until someone finally freaked out and begged the driver to hit the gas and get the hell out of there.

That's Lake Herman Road. It's a lonely place. Always has been, and it's no different now.

But Halloween is different these days. In Vallejo, it's no longer about trick-or-treaters. There's a new tradition now. On Halloween night, more than a few Vallejo teenagers drive down a quiet country road, following the same route that David Faraday's '61 Rambler took all those years ago. They pass the old Borges ranch house, dip down through the stunted oaks that line the road by the still lake, and they park at a spot where rolling hills cut off the lights from town...where it's so dark that you can actually see how black the night is, and how many stars there are in the sky.

It's a spot where a boy just their age took a bullet behind his ear on a cold December night...where a girl couldn't run fast enough to escape her own death...where a man turned his back on the both of them and drove away in the darkness.

BLACK LEATHER KITES

The riderless Toro mower rounded second base and headed for third, and from his perch atop the pitcher's mound Dennis Wichita eyed the mechanical beast the same way a man stranded on a desert island eyes a hungry shark. At least that's the way the scene looked to Deputy Chavez, who admired Gary Larson's *Far Side* cartoons.

"All this one needs," Bernardo Chavez said, "is a palm tree and a duck."

A dust devil swirled across the baseline and chalk powdered the deputy's Nocona boots. The Toro motored toward home plate, coughing like an aged DH. Then the rampaging mower suddenly changed course, and the trio of flashlights duct-taped to its chassis illuminated Dennis Wichita.

"C'mon, Nardo!" Wichita's expression melted from simple concern to full-bore hysteria. "Jesus H. Christ, c'mon!"

The deputy's fingers danced over the grip of his .357. The Toro had red fenders and a blue body, a custom paint-job that left little doubt in Nardo's mind as to the identity of the mower's owner. But reason reared its ugly head, and his gun remained in its holster. Nardo didn't want to piss off Letty, though a dead mower would serve Bill right for putting a relative through this kind of grief on the third watch.

Nardo Chavez charged the Toro. He was a stocky man, 209 pounds the last time he'd bothered to tangle with a scale, and he mounted the mower gracelessly, cutting the power just as the machine skirted the mound.

The deputy leaned against the steering wheel and worked up his Jack Webb voice. "Let's hear it, Wich."

The junkman popped a Lifesaver between his thin lips and endeavored to stay downwind of the deputy. "Damnedest thing, Nardo. I was heading home from the junkyard when I seen the lights. I thought some bikers were tearing up the field…figured it for a Halloween prank, y'know. Anyway, I helped coach one of the teams last season—Ascot Funeral Home Panthers, we finished in third place—and I sure don't want my boys fielding balls out of a bunch of tire tracks next year, so I pulled over and started hollering. Just about then a truck pulled out from behind the equipment shed. Damned thing headed right for me and creased my fender, and about the time I scraped my chin up off the seat cushions I seen—and I swear to God this next part is true, 'cause it's a full moon tonight and I could see just as plain as day—anyway, what I seen in the back of that truck was a bunch of boys all dressed up in hoods and such. And you know how windy it is tonight and all, and when I seen what happened next I figured it had to be a prank for sure 'cause the bastards let loose with a half-dozen kites right off the truck-bed while they tore down Highway 63!"

The deputy laughed. "I think it's time for you to toe the baseline. Or you can try lobbing a few quick ones over home plate…see if you can strike me out. Take your pick."

"Shit, Nardo…."

A dry breeze drove a wave of dust across the field. Nardo squinted, fighting the urge to rub his eyes. "Okay, let's try this again, with some ground rules this time. Lights I can buy. I can buy a truck sideswiping you. Hell, tonight I can even buy guys in hoods and you being sober. But box kites? C'mon, Wich."

"Not box kites." The junkman's hands went as wide as an imaginative fisherman's. "They were big enough, all right. And they were made of something heavy and shiny, like leather. Black leather. But they looked like.... Aw shit, the damn things looked like bats."

"Bats. Uh-huh. How about the truck then? It look like the Batmobile?"

"Shit no. Dodge."

"You sure?"

"Dodge Dakota. I know a goddamn Dodge Dakota when I see one, Nardo. Same truck that I'm driving. A damn good one. For an Eye-talian, that Iacocca—"

"Spare me." The deputy shined his flashlight across the field, pausing when the beam illuminated a blue-and-red baseball cap that had been ripped to bits by the rampaging Toro just short of second base. "Blue-and-red truck?" he asked.

"Yeah. How'd you know?"

The deputy flashed his light on the blue-and-red mower, then on the shredded blue-and-red cap. "I'm a trained observer," he said.

Nardo sent Wichita to check the concession stand and the equipment shed for signs of a break-in. Then he thumbed the extender mic fastened to his left epaulet and hailed dispatch by way of the handpack radio attached to his belt. "71SAM1 here,"

he said, and Sylvia Martin acknowledged. "Put me out of service, Sylvia—investigating suspicious circumstances at the little league field. Let's go code 4 with this one. We'll let 71NORA1 enjoy his nap, wherever he might be." Sylvia laughed and Nardo signed off, happy to get a jab in at Ron Allen, the deputy who was working the northern end of the county.

Wichita hadn't returned. Nardo found a pay phone behind the bleachers and was embarrassed when he had to look up Letty's number in the phone book. Of course, he flipped to "Chavez" before he remembered that she'd be under "Bleu" these days. Her voice was groggy with sleep. "Billy, it's one o'clock."

"Not Billy, *niña*...it's only your big bad big brother."

"Nardo! What's up? Don't tell me something happened to—"

Not wanting to answer the obvious question, Nardo cut her off with a half-truth. "Looks like my least-favorite brother-in-law left some of his precious equipment here at the little league field. I thought I'd save him a trip, if you can tell me where I might find him."

"It's hard to say. With this heat wave and the full moon, he decided to work late, when it's coolest. He left here about nine tonight, but he could be almost anywhere because he's got to change the timers on all the watering systems he services. You know—daylight savings time ends tonight."

"Tell me about it. I've got to pull an extra hour of mandatory."

"Sorry I can't help you." Letty's voice brightened. "You can always drop Billy's stuff here at the house. I can make some coffee. Bill left a slice of peach pie in the fridge, and there's some Häagen-Dazs in the freezer...vanilla, I think. It's been a long time, *hermano*."

Nardo almost swore. His baby sister baked peach pie for the bastard! Bill Bleu sure as hell didn't deserve that. And they ate designer ice cream, too. Hell, they were probably doing well enough to afford that imported beer with the tin-foil jackets. The landscaping business must be pretty damn solid.

"Well?" Letty said. "How about it?"

"Naw. I think I'll just hunt up your husband. Who knows, he could be stumbling around with amnesia or something." Nardo sighed. "And I'll pass on what I'm sure would be a damn fine cup of non-instant coffee, and the pie, and the ice cream, and the truffles and finger sandwiches and whatever other goodies the maids and butlers didn't get into today."

"Watching your weight, El Bandito?" she teased. "Making a comeback?"

"Your husband wishes," Nardo said, and he hung up laughing.

El Bandito. It had been a long time since anyone had called him that. Nardo walked to second base and scooped up the tattered cap. Before he could straighten up, another blast of hot wind sprayed dust in his eyes. He swore, squinting, not rubbing because he remembered all too well the doctor's warning about rubbing an eye that had suffered a detached retina.

The injury had come in his biggest fight, a bout with Carl "The Truth" Williams, who at the time possessed the best jab in the heavyweight division outside of Larry Holmes. Best thumb, too. Anyway, the detached ret had ended the career of Bernardo "El Bandito" Chavez, an in-your-face boxer with a good left hook who had KO'd a string of fringe contenders.

While the doctors had been able to repair his eye, they had also recommended that he retire. Nardo had taken their advice, and since then no one had succeeded in finding him another career that satisfied his lust for designer ice cream and foil-sheathed beer. Lately, he settled for the in-store brand when it came to ice cream, and his beer of choice was canned and the special of the week.

At least he'd earned enough from his loss to Williams to buy a new house in his hometown and a used Firebird. And time. Time to think things through for the first time in his life. And when the money ran out he was done thinking; he took the law enforcement exams at the county office and now here he was. A deputy. An upstanding member of the community. But drawing county pay meant that luxuries came few and far between—his Noconas were on their third set of heels and three of the four speakers in his Firebird were long dead—and the things some people called him these days made him long for the days when they'd called him "El Bandito."

At first. Bill had pushed for a comeback. Training Nardo was the only job he'd ever had, and he wasn't happy about losing his one-and-only client. "Look at Sugar Ray Leonard," he'd whined. "He didn't quit when they fixed his eye. He made big money afterward."

"The gravy train's done run its course. Bill. You'd better get yourself a job, because if you don't take care of my sister I'll put your ass in a sling." Those had been the deputy's exact words.

Fuck it. Nardo rubbed his eyes and felt blessed relief from the dust. He dribbled in some eye drops as an afterthought and was still blinking when a blurry Dennis Wichita came jogging toward him.

"You were right!" Wichita called. "There is something missing! The equipment shed was busted open, and the chalker is gone!"

"The chalker?"

Wichita pointed to the indistinct first baseline, which disappeared under a cloud of dust. "You know—the machine we use to line the field."

Nardo took Wichita's keys and told him he'd be back in a hour or two with a full report, suggesting not too subtly that Lee Iacocca had designed the seat of the Dodge Dakota especially for sleeping off tough nights. Then the deputy thumbed his extender mic and arranged a meeting with Ron Allen at the Ascot Funeral Home parking lot.

After Nardo related the story of the missing chalker and a good bit of family history, Ron asked, "Is your brother-in-law drunk, or is he just naturally insane?"

"Who knows? Maybe the whole thing is a Halloween prank. Bill and his buddies might do something crazy if they got a real snootful. They might be out there this minute chalking dirty words on decent folks' lawns."

"Halloween night." Ron laughed. "And a full moon, to boot. Shit, I hate working mids. The only time to deal with nuts is in the light of day."

"If then."

They decided to soft-pedal it for a while. When they found Bill, they'd try to talk sense to him, convince him that the thing to do would be to pay for Wich's truck repair and return the chalker. And maybe skip a couple of the county's field maintenance bills, too, just to show that he was genuinely embarrassed about the whole thing. If Bill did that, and if he was very nice about it, maybe they wouldn't worry about the 459, the 2002, and the big bad deuce rap. It sure as hell would save all concerned a whole bunch of paperwork, and Dennis Wichita had already told Nardo that the last thing he wanted to do was deal with his insurance company. Again.

Nardo got behind the wheel of the patrol car and headed for the county line, thinking about Bill's biggest contracts, the places he was likely to visit first. He'd start with the cemetery, then work his way back toward the heart of the county. Soon he found himself thinking about Häagen-Dazs and foil-wrapped beers and steak dinners—thick filet mignons smothered with mushrooms and garlic and red onions—but he couldn't work up a good head of jealousy over Bill's success. His brother-in-law was a real entrepreneur. Two years ago he'd started out with a mail-order book called *How to Earn $50 an Hour with a Pickup Truck*, and now he was....

Hell, now he was driving around drunk while his loony buddies flew black leather kites off of his truck-bed.

Nardo eased the blue-and-white Dodge Diplomat onto Old Howard Road, careful to avoid the many potholes that dotted the blacktop. Up ahead, a blue-and-red pickup was parked on the sloping shoulder. Nardo killed his lights as he pulled in behind it.

Stepping onto the gravel shoulder, he took his nunchaku from the inside door panel. When he was a teenager, he had seen every Bruce Lee movie that had played at the Visalia Drive-In at least a dozen times, and he'd been sold on the preferred weapon of Okinawan rice farmers ever since, even though his police training with the chucks had disappointed him, concentrating on wrist locks rather than elegant flourishes and passes. Still, he had seen many a perp freeze at the very sight of them, and he thought that the chucks were a hell of a lot more intimidating than the nightsticks most cops carried or the tonfas favored by the California Highway Patrol.

Nardo checked the truck. Nothing. He tried contacting Sylvia Martin with his extender mic, but he was too far from the station's repeater and the signal was miserably weak, so he called in his position using the patrol car's more powerful radio.

Once again, code 4. Once again, investigating suspicious circumstances.

The full moon shone a chalky white-blue, the color of an oyster. Nardo hustled quietly across a weed-choked drainage ditch and through a tangle of scrub oak that partially circled the cemetery fence, glad for the moon because it made his flashlight unnecessary. He started to swing open the rusty gate before he saw the men, and the squealing hinges would have given him away for sure if not for the loud chanting that began at the same instant.

"The darkness, the darkness,
The light, the light,
At midnight, at midnight,
On Halloween night."

Nardo dipped low, taking cover behind a leafy oak. He'd nearly walked right into it.

There were about ten of them, and just like Dennis Wichita had said, they were flying kites. Nardo saw three bat-shaped silhouettes darting and diving before the bright moon, though it didn't appear that any of the men were holding kite reels or paying much attention to the aerial acrobatics.

One of the men came forward, pushing something that looked like an old lawn mower. The chalker. The man bent low and jammed his arm into the machine, first to the wrist, then the forearm, then the elbow, and when he stood up, in the brief moment before the heavy, leathery sleeve of his robe descended, it appeared that he had lost his right arm.

Nardo inched back toward his patrol car. It was a trick, he told himself. Damn spooky, but just a trick. Still, he wanted to call Ron Allen for backup.

The one-armed man pulled another man forward, and a third man started to push the chalker, circling the first two. Nardo's hand drifted to his gun.

Darkness... Light... Midnight.... There was a sudden series of sharp beeps—someone's wristwatch signaling the hour—and a circle of flame exploded between Nardo and the crowd. Inside the circle, two ashen faces swam against a roiling red-orange background, and Nardo immediately recognized Bill as one of the men.

A glint of metal amid the flames. A knife arcing above Bill's head.

Bill and the other man disappeared behind a curtain of sparks.

Nardo banged through the gate and sprinted through a tombstone obstacle course. The sparks were flickering low, but rising curls of mushroom-colored smoke hid his progress from the chanting men. Again, he went for his gun, hesitated just an instant at the thought of an elaborate prank, and instead pulled his chucks and dove for the circle just as a dozen sprinklers fountained water over the cemetery lawn.

The flames were quenched almost instantly. The edge of the circle glowed orange, and as Nardo passed over it he saw Bill again, saw the cartoon-like outline of a bat glowing red on the grass at his brother-in-law's feet. Then the wind kicked out of Nardo's lungs and he felt like he was elbowing through something alive, like you'd feel if you were flailing around in the guts of a whale, and the chanting that boomed in his ears suddenly increased in pitch until it became a shrieking whine. But all he could think about was getting there, getting to the knife that even now was descending toward Bill's heart, and he whipped the chucks around the one-armed man's wrist and levered the two sticks together.

There was a sound like an ear of corn being stripped from its stalk as the man's wrist powdered. His hand fell away. The knife landed at the point of the bat-design's left ear.

"Jesus." Nardo pulled his gun as the tall man dropped to his knees. "Jesus!"

The screeching whine screamed to a deafening pitch. Nardo whirled toward the robed men. A few of them crouched at the perimeter of the circle, dying beneath cascading fountains of water, puddling to nothing like outcasts from *The Wizard of Oz*. Nardo was ready to surrender to a feeling of crazy relief—Bill already had and was laughing heartily at the wild sight of dissolving devil cultists—but then Nardo saw that several others had escaped the sprinklers; they had transformed themselves into huge black bats, not kites, and now they flapped leathery wings and dived before the full moon, staying well away from the sprinklers.

Hot wind blasted through the circle, a scorching twister driven by the circling bats. A black shadow washed over the moon, and Nardo's mind couldn't accept the reality of the dark silhouette until his patrol car came crashing down, shattering marble tombstones and collapsing a section of wrought-iron fence. The creatures that had dropped the car darted to the edge of the cemetery, and just as Nardo noticed that the water from the sprinklers wasn't penetrating the circle, the sprinklers sputtered and dripped off to nothing.

Bill swore. "Those bastards turned off the timers. They're gonna come for us now, Nardo. Christ, do something!"

Before the last sentence had issued from Bill's lips, a huge bat dived toward him, its steely incisors dripping saliva. Nardo fired just as the creature dodged up toward the moon, and then another sound cut at the men inside the circle, the sound of a bullet ricocheting off metal. Three tiny flashes exploded at the circle's perimeter, and the bullet fell spent on the singed grass before Nardo could begin to react.

With the stump of his wrist, the one-armed man rapped on the invisible barrier. Three echoing knocks, like knuckles on a empty oil drum. Then the man laughed, and his laughter increased in pitch until it was an ugly shriek.

Bill snatched up the cultist's knife and moved to finish him, but Nardo held him back. "Let me go, damn it. The bastard tried to kill me!" Bill pointed the knife at the singed grass beneath his feet. "And besides, look what the fucker's done to my Kentucky bluegrass!"

They couldn't leave the circle. None of the bat-things could enter, though they kept trying. The creatures battered the invisible barrier like moths drawn to a well-lighted window. As soon as the blistering wind dried the grass, the things landed and slammed their furry bodies against the barrier, folding their wings and using the tips of their long, bony fingers as pole vaults. Hell, Nardo had never seen a bat pole-vault over a tombstone before. That was weird enough, but the snot trails they left on the invisible wall when they bashed it with their rubbery pink snouts were just plain disgusting.

Okay. They couldn't get in, and Nardo and Bill couldn't get out. But the scorching whirlwind could pass straight on through. It burned Nardo's lungs, hotter now than it had been at the ballpark, though he couldn't understand how that was possible.

The one-armed man stood at the opposite side of the circle. He refused to meet Nardo's gaze. Bill sat in the circle's center, nervously tugging brown clumps of Kentucky bluegrass, the knife cradled in his lap. It had been about a half an hour, Nardo figured, since they'd been trapped.

Nardo spoke first. "This boy is pretty quiet, isn't he. Bill? I mean, considering all the excitement."

"Now, hell yeah, but you should've heard him earlier. As soon as his boys pulled me off my mower he starts in with 'All glory to Satan' and some shit about the full moon and Halloween and sacrifice and rebirth, and they're all bowing down to him like he's the Grand Poobah or something. C'mon, Nardo, we already know the bastard ain't human. He lost a good chunk of his anatomy to the chalker, and he ain't even bleeding." Bill quit pulling grass and gripped the knife. "Why don't you just let me whack the fucker's head off and we'll see if he's still so cheery!"

"Naw," Nardo said. "That happens, maybe we're stuck here forever. Our friend here is probably the only one who can tell us the way out of this fix we're in. Maybe he's got some little way we can help him out, and we can just call this whole evening a standoff." Nardo stared down at Bill. "Now, be a good boy and give me that knife before you get us into trouble."

Protesting, Bill did as he was told, and Nardo tucked the blade under his belt, noting with satisfaction the cultist's appreciative smile. Nardo returned the grin, then winked at Bill. Good cop, bad cop. It had worked before. It was probably a brand new scam to a werebat, or whatever the hell this guy was, and maybe it would buy them some time.

Nardo pointed his pistol at the cultist's severed hand. "Sorry about that. Bet it hurt like hell."

"Not much."

"Well, I guess it'll put a crimp in your human sacrificing for a while. Damn shame, I suppose. I hope it doesn't get the man downstairs all pissed off at you." Nardo wiped sweat from his brow. "Look, I've read *Rosemary's Baby* and I've seen *Brotherhood of Satan*. Isn't this the point where you're supposed to offer me three wishes, or immortality, or something?"

"That could be arranged."

"C'mon, Nardo, let's ice this fucker—"

"Put a sock in it. Bill." Nardo slipped his .357 into its holster and raised his empty hands to the cultist. "Do tell," he invited.

"Well, Sheriff—"

"Don't gild the lily. Make it *Deputy*."

"Very well, Deputy. There is one way out of this situation, and that is to raise that knife and plunge it into your friend's heart."

"I wouldn't call him a friend. He's my brother-in-law. But say I do that little thing. Then the walls come tumbling down and you just let me go?"

"That would be telling."

"Well, do I have some time to think it over, at least?"

With the stump of his wrist, the cultist pointed to the edge of the circle. The dust was dry now, powdery, and the swirling wind was beginning to thin the boundary. "Even now the dust of my life scatters. See? My brothers have stirred Satan's breath. That is the only thing that keeps us alive, the only thing that can penetrate the circle until the dust is charged with the blood of the living. And that must happen soon, for when the circle is no more, I will be no more. And then my brothers will be most unhappy, for you will have sentenced them to death. You two won't last an instant against them."

Bill inhaled deeply. "Satan's breath, huh? My ass. I'm a Christian man, and I can breathe this air just fine."

Nardo shook his head. "Well, Bill, maybe God doesn't approve of you transporting devil cults in your Dodge Dakota. I don't recall anything about that in the Ten Commandments, but maybe it didn't make the short list."

"Levity in the face of doom is admirable, Deputy. But if you're going to make a decision, you'd best make it soon."

Nardo whistled. "Kind of one of those moral dilemma things, huh?" He ran his finger over the blade. "I just have one other question, then. If I do this for you, will I be flapping around for all eternity?"

"There are worse things."

Nardo returned the knife to Bill. "Don't get any ideas about turning the tables on me, Billy. You sprout bat wings, you'll have one hell of a time scratching your ass."

The cultist whispered something, but his words were eclipsed by the angry shrieks of his winged brethren.

Nardo pulled the one-armed man to his feet. The bats hovered at the edge of the circle, furiously beating their wings, kicking up the powdery remnants of the cultist's arm, uncovering the scorched grass below.

Nardo lashed out. A left jab. A hard one. The one-armed man's nose collapsed; his cheeks cracked and caved in, and Nardo pulled his second punch as the man hit the edge of the circle and crumbled within the folds of his leathery robe.

"If you would've hit Carl Williams like that, we wouldn't be in this fix," Bill said. "'Course, Williams had two hands and could hit back."

"Don't start." Nardo grabbed the cultist's robe and shook it at Bill's feet. Bits and pieces hit the ground. Some bounced. Some didn't.

"Look, I don't want any part of this," Bill whispered.

Nardo grabbed the cultist's withered cock, powdered it in his fist, and sprinkled it at the edge of the circle. He glanced at Bill. "I did that little bit because I didn't want to hear you complain. Now get busy, and I mean directly."

"Even if we grind this sucker up, he ain't gonna last forever. Those furry bastards will just keep on flapping, and pretty soon we'll be right back where we are right now."

"I don't plan to be here all night. Sylvia Martin knows where I am. I can't reach her with my handpack, but pretty soon she'll send Ron Allen along to check on me, and—"

The sound of a siren rose in the distance. Nardo fumbled with his extender mic. Ron was in range, and he hailed him easily, the signal strong and clear.

"No, this isn't a gag, Ron.... Yes, we've got a dangerous situation here.... I guess the most I can say right now is that hostages have been taken, and I want to hear a hell of a lot more sirens before I see any lights."

If the bats understood, they didn't panic, and they didn't break away to pursue Ron Allen. Instead they flapped, screeched, and circled, intent only on their fallen brother and the men who had killed him. Nardo couldn't help watching the things. He knew that they were consumed by the need for revenge, and he figured that the hunger for his blood was probably the only thing that kept them from powdering away to nothing.

But they couldn't last forever, not without the ceremony. That was plain enough. Satan's breath tore thatches of red-brown fur from their chests. Shingles of leathery flesh drifted over the cemetery like falling leaves. The bats' anger was stirring the wind and speeding their destruction. It was a race they couldn't win.

Nardo bent down and helped his brother-in-law. A gray cloud mushroomed up from the cultist's crumbling hand. Blinded, Nardo rubbed his eyes, but Bill pulled Nardo's hands away.

"Watch yourself. Here, use my bandana, but be careful."

Nardo cleaned his eyes and almost said something stupid and sentimental about blood being thicker than water.

Bill beat him to it, then added, "I'm sorry about that Carl Williams crack. Really."

"If you treat me to a slice of peach pie when this is over, and maybe toss in some Häagen-Dazs and a couple bottles of good beer as an appetizer, I'll think about forgiving you."

"Sure thing." Bill coughed as he reinforced the circle. "Really, this ain't so bad. Hell of a lot easier than installing a new sprinkler system."

"It shouldn't be long now," Nardo said. "When we make our break, do you want to take the knife or the chucks?"

Bill thought it over as he powdered the cultist's head and siphoned the dust through his fingers. "Shit, Nardo, how about you be a real sport and let me take the .357?"

Shaking his head, Nardo handed over the gun.

Headlights bloomed out on 63. The bats didn't seem to notice. Nardo and Bill stepped to the center of the circle, back to back, and the chalky boundary dusted around their boots.

Nardo brandished the chucks, stirring a breeze all his own, and cocked the weapon over his shoulder.

"Batter up," he said.

TREATS

Monsters stalked the supermarket aisles.

Maddie pushed the squeaky-wheeled cart past a pack of werewolves, smiling when they growled at her because that was the polite thing to do. She couldn't help staring at the bright eyes inside the plastic masks. Brown eyes, blue and green eyes. Human eyes. Not the eyes that she couldn't see. Not the black eyes that stared at her from Jimmy's face, so cold, ordering her here and there without a glint of compassion or love.

"Jimmy, get away from that candy!"

Maddie covered her mouth, fearful that she'd spoken. No, she hadn't said anything. Besides, Jimmy was at home with them. He'd said that they were preparing for Operation Trojan Horse and he had to speak to them before—

"Jimmy, I'm telling you for the last time...."

A little ghoul clutching a trick-or-treat bag scampered down the aisle. He tore at the wrapping of a Snickers bar and gobbled a big bite before his mother caught his tattered collar.

"I warned you, young man," she said, snatching away the bright-orange treat sack. "You're not going to eat this candy all at once and make yourself sick. You're allowed one piece a day, remember? That way your treats will last for a long, long time."

Maddie saw the little boy's shoulders slump. Her Jimmy had done the same thing last Halloween when Maddie had given him a similar speech, except her Jimmy had been a sad-faced clown, not a ghoul.

And not a general. Not *their* general.

Maddie raised her hand, as if she could wave off the boy's mother before she made the same mistake Maddie had made a year earlier. She saw lipstick smears on her fingers and imagined what her face must look like. It had been so long since they'd allowed her to wear cosmetics that she'd made a mess of herself without realizing it. The boy's mother would see that, and she wouldn't listen. She'd rush away with her son before Maddie could warn her.

Defeated, the boy stared down at his ghoul-face mirrored in the freshly waxed floor. His mother crumpled his trick-or-treat bag closed, and the moment slowed. Maddie saw herself reaching into her shopping cart, watched her lipstick-smeared fingers tear open a bag of Milk Duds and fling the little yellow boxes down the aisle in a slow, scattering arc. She saw the other Jimmy's mother yelling at her, the boxes bouncing, the big store windows behind the little ghoul and the iron-gray clouds boiling outside. Wind-driven leaves the color of old skin crackling against the glass.

And then Maddie was screaming at the little ghoul. "Eat your candy! Eat it now! Don't let them come after it!"

She paid for the Milk Duds, of course, and for all the other candy that she had heaped into the shopping cart. The manager didn't complain. Maddie knew that the ignorant man only wanted her out of his store.

He thought that she was crazy.

Papery leaves clawed at her ankles as she loaded the candy into the back of the station wagon. She smiled, remembering the other Jimmy, the ghoul Jimmy, gobbling Milk Duds. Other monsters had joined in the feast. Werewolves, Frankensteins, zombies. Maddie prayed that they'd all have awful stomachaches. Then they'd stay home, snuggled in front of their television sets. They wouldn't come knocking at her door tonight. They'd be safe from her Jimmy and his army.

Maddie climbed into the station wagon and slammed the door. She pretended not to notice Jimmy's friends in the back seat. It was easy, because she couldn't see them, couldn't see their black eyes. But she could feel their presence nonetheless.

Slowly, Maddie drove home. Little monsters stood on front porches and watched the gray sky, waiting intently for true darkness, when they would descend on the neighborhood in search of what Jimmy wanted to give them. Maddie glanced in the rearview mirror at the grocery bags in the back of the station wagon. Even in brown paper, even wrapped in plastic, she could smell the sugar. It was the only smell she knew anymore, and she tasted it in the back of her throat.

God, she'd been tasting it for a year now.

"*Mommy,*" Jimmy had cried, "you said my candy would last. Now look at it. Look at *them*. They ruined it. I want new candy. I want it now!"

But Jimmy's whining had been a lie. Maddie knew that now. Jimmy hadn't wanted the candy. *They* had wanted it, and they'd coaxed Jimmy into getting it for them. And they scared her, even if they didn't scare her son. They'd always scared her.

Because they were everywhere. In the cupboards. Under the floor. In the garden and under the rim of the toilet seat. Maddie's house swelled with them. And when she went to work, they were there, too, watching her through the windows. Black eyes she couldn't see, staring. Through the winter cold, through the summer heat, they were always there. Studying her. Never resting.

They had her son, too. He had a million fathers now, all who cared for him more than the man who'd given him his face and his last name before disappearing beneath a wave of unpaid bills. They nested in Jimmy's room and traveled in his lunch box. Jimmy took them places and showed them things. He taught them about the town, and they told him how smart he was. They made him a general and swore to obey his commands.

Maddie pulled into the driveway and cut the engine. She sat in the quiet car, dreading the house. Inside, Jimmy's legions waited. Jimmy waited, too. But Jimmy wasn't a sad-faced clown anymore. Now he was a great leader, and he was about to attack.

The sky rumbled.

Heavy raindrops splattered the windshield.

Maddie almost smiled but caught herself just in time. She glanced in the rearview mirror and pretended to wipe at her smeared lipstick, but really she was looking for Jimmy's spies.

She wished that she could see their eyes.

Jimmy was in the basement, telling the story of the Trojan horse. They stood at attention in orderly black battalions, listening to every word. Maddie didn't know how they tolerated it. Jimmy had told them the story at least a hundred times.

"The candy's upstairs, Jimmy. I left it on the kitchen table."

Jimmy thumbed the brim of a military cap that was much too large for his head. He'd made Maddie buy the cap at an army surplus store, and it was the smallest size available. "I'll grow into it." That's what he'd said, smiling, but he wasn't smiling now.

Maddie managed a grin. "The candy, Jimmy. You remember—"

"Of course I remember! I only wish that you'd remember to call me the right thing!"

"I'm sorry, General." Maddie straightened. "The candy—the supplies—are upstairs in the mess hall."

Jimmy seemed pleased. "Very good. Bring the supplies down here, and we'll begin Operation Trojan Horse."

Maddie stared at the black sea on the cement floor, imagining a million eyes focused on her. She wouldn't walk among them. Not when she could see them clearly, not when she could feel them scuttling over her feet.

"I don't want to do that," she said.

The boy's lips twisted into a cruel smile. "Maybe you'd rather have me send a few squads to your bedroom tonight, like the last time you disobeyed a direct order. You won't get much sleep with a jillion little feet crawling all over you...."

"Jimmy!" She stared at him, revolted by his black insect eyes, and then turned away.

She got the candy.

Jimmy used a penknife to make tiny holes in the packages. His troops climbed inside, listening to their leader talk of conquest and the Trojan Horse and the birth of a new order. He told them the best places to hide in a house and reminded the scouts that he must be kept informed at all times concerning the progress of their mission.

And when they were all in place, why then...

Silently, Maddie climbed the stairs. Rainwater ran down the front window, drooling from the rusty gutters above. The street outside was slick and black. The sidewalks were empty, gray; a flotilla of fallen leaves swam in the cement gutters. Maddie watched the leaves and imagined hundreds of little monsters washed into their homes by a great wave.

She looked down and saw her son's face mirrored in the window. His reflection was smeared with rain, sad, his straight lips twisted into a dripping frown, his black eyes deep pools overflowing high cheekbones. He exhaled sharply and the image fogged over.

"They just told me," he whispered. "It took them a long time to get out of the car. I guess you think that was pretty smart, closing the vents and all."

Maddie said nothing. She stared at the foggy spot on the window. *Just a glimpse*, she thought. *Just a glimpse, but it was a clown's face I saw.*

"I never thought about this." Jimmy stared out at the rain. "They aren't coming, are they?"

"Not tonight."

Jimmy whispered, "Not tonight, troops. Operation Trojan Horse is scrubbed."

Maddie took a deep breath, hating the air, hating the stink of sugar. She thought about the little clown she'd seen mirrored in the rain-washed window, and she thought about the other Jimmy, the little ghoul, safe and dry in front of a TV set.

Tiny antennae probed Maddie's heel. Tiny feet, sticky with chocolate, marched over her toes.

The rain came harder now, in sheets. Jimmy brushed his troops away from his mother's feet. He rose and took her hand. Mirrored in the window, his lips were straight, his jaw firm.

God, it's been so long since he touched me, she thought, but she said, "Jimmy, let's watch television."

He nodded, studying the rain, not really listening.

His eyes narrowed until Maddie couldn't see them anymore.

"Next year," he said, his grip tightening.

THREE DOORS

When Halloween rolled around that year, Johnny Meyers painted his right hand black.

Of course, that right hand didn't really belong to Johnny. It was made of rubber, and he'd only had it three months. Brought it back from the war with him. Doesn't matter which war. They're all the same.

Now, Johnny didn't paint his hand black because he wanted a costume. Sure, it was Halloween, but he didn't care about that. It was more like he wanted that hand to do some things for him—things he couldn't manage if it were pink and clean and ordinary.

So Johnny got out some black enamel he'd used to paint model cars when he was a kid. He loosened up a stiff brush in a jar of thinner, and he painted the hand from its fake fingertips to its socketed rubber wrist. Then he sat and watched a monster movie while the paint dried. Trick or treaters knocked on the front door that Johnny never answered, and Frankenstein and the Wolf Man went at it on the TV. But Johnny Meyers paid no attention. He sat there as still as could be, cradling that rubber hand in his lap.

An hour ticked by. The drying paint stretched like a new skin over Johnny's prosthetic hand, pulling those rubber fingers tight, curling them into a fist sealed up by a rubber thumb.

That was all right with Johnny.

Tonight he needed a fist.

Because a fist was built for knocking.

Now, maybe that's a little hard to believe. Not the part about a fist being built for knocking, but the part about a rubber hand curling into a fist because of a little black paint. But, hey... it doesn't really matter if you believe it or not. That's the way it happened. You can go ahead and fill in the blanks yourself if you need to. Figure someone cast a bucket of mojo over that fake hand while Johnny was in the hospital. Figure that a dying patient sweated some magic into that hand before he kicked off, and the folks in the PT unit decided to save the government a few bucks and pass on that five-fingered hunk of rubber to Johnny. Hell, you can figure the damn hand came from some haunted curio shop over on the far side of *The Twilight Zone* if you want to.

Doesn't matter to me how you explain it.

See, I'm not here to draw you a diagram.

I'm just here to tell you a story.

So when Johnny got up out of his chair, he knew exactly what that mojo hand could do for him. He'd been thinking about it all week long—listening to dry leaves churn out there in the black October night…eyeing those fat pumpkins waiting for knives on all those neatly swept porches over in town…

watching spookshows on his little excuse for a TV when sleep wouldn't come.

What Johnny was thinking about was the power that painted hand would hold tonight, on Halloween, when witches and broomsticks and all that other crap that goes bump in the night holds sway. And what Johnny's brain told him was this: his mojo hand would give him three magic knocks on three ordinary doors. And it didn't matter who waited behind those doors—every one of them would open for Johnny Meyers, and whoever waited on the other side would be his to command.

And I know what you're thinking now. Sure—I've heard of "The Monkey's Paw." Who the hell hasn't? A bucket of sour mojo, three wishes going bad, a dead guy knocking on his momma's door...all that. But that was W. W. Jacobs' story. This one's mine, and I'll play it my way. It's about a rubber hand that's painted black, and a guy named Johnny, and three doors he'll be knocking on before midnight rolls around.

So Johnny moved on—the screen door banged shut behind him, heavy footfalls thudded across the porch, dry leaves crackled beneath his boots as he crossed the yard to the gravel driveway.

Johnny's pickup waited by the mailbox. It wasn't much to look at. More rust than steel—a little bit like Johnny himself.

A yank courtesy of Johnny's real hand, and the door ratcheted open like an old man's jaw.

Johnny climbed behind the wheel, started the engine, and notched that sucker into gear.

Lucky for Johnny, the truck was an automatic. Would have been hell shifting with a rubber hand if he'd had a manual transmission. But Johnny's truck was easy—the only thing he'd really had to do as far as conversion was tighten down a clamp that attached a little knob to the steering wheel. After that, all he had to do was grab hold of that knob with his good hand, and he could make his turns one-handed.

Johnny headed up a two-lane road. Country—not many lights out there unless you knew where to look for them. The truck's radio didn't work, and neither did the heater. The cab was cold enough to make a rattler sleep through the whole damn winter without feeling a thing. Johnny himself didn't feel it much. He was a big guy. Lots of meat on him—minus that right hand, of course.

It was a familiar road, and it brought familiar memories. There were lots of things Johnny remembered about the way things were before the war. Lots of things he'd forgotten, too… but, hey, a couple of grenades send you twenty feet in the air and take a couple pounds of skin and bone off you in the bargain, you'd figure it would shake a few parts loose in your brainpan, too.

That's the way it was with Johnny. Of the stuff he remembered, most of it was good. Like drives with Elena on nights like this. Banging around country roads in the old pickup, just the two of them. Driving down to the river where the water seemed to run cold and clear any time of year. Finding the moon down there waiting above the trees like some kind of searchlight, and finding the shadows that could hide them from it.

Laughter in the dark. Just the two of them. That was the way Johnny liked remembering it. Those nights by the river, and other nights before he'd gone away. That was what he had. See, Johnny hadn't seen Elena since he'd come home. Mostly, it was because of her parents. They had their reasons. In fact, her dad had Johnny over for a beer when he first got home. Sat him down at the table. No one else in the house—not Elena, not her mom. The old man wasn't what you'd call talkative but there were words, the kind that barely peak above a whisper. He explained things to Johnny, told him why he couldn't see Elena anymore. But the words didn't matter to Johnny. For him, those words were curled fists, banging away on a closed door inside...one that was locked and bolted and wouldn't open for any-goddamn-one.

But Johnny didn't want to think about that. He rolled down the window, searching for those other memories. The good ones. The side mirror caught the moonlight, but he didn't try to hide from it at all. No. This night was different. He'd do his hiding later, when Elena was with him.

He drove on. The cold air combed through his hair, and he caught the smell of a dirt road still damp with the first rain of the season mixed up with the scent of the wild apple orchard that stretched from the county road to the banks of the cold, clear river below.

The night was crisp and tart with the smell of ripening apples. Johnny didn't like it much. Somehow it made him think of Elena's father, and the things he'd said after Johnny came home. So Johnny rolled up the window and went searching for more pleasant scents that lingered in his memory.

Like roses.

Elena loved roses.

Johnny brought them for her all the time.

By any other name, they were just as sweet.

That was Johnny's first stop. A little florist shop downtown.

The truck door creaked open and Johnny stepped out. It was almost midnight now. Pretty deserted on the streets. He walked across the parking lot, black rubber hand swinging at his side, heart pounding so hard he couldn't hear his own footsteps. Giddy as a little kid. Because the whole deal was getting too close now, playing out in Johnny's head like quick-cut scenes in those late night creepshows he'd been watching all week. But these scenes weren't creepshows at all. Uh-uh. No way.

These scenes were sweet. Johnny saw his beater of a pickup truck, that rusty bed heaped with more roses than anyone could imagine. The perfume washed over him, almost smothered him as he drove up the little dirt road that led to Elena's place, and he imagined her expression when she caught sight of him with all those roses—

At the florist shop door, his reflection waited on the glass.

He raised his hand, put black rubber knuckle to its twin.

And he waited some more.

Turned out, he waited a long damn time.

The door didn't open. Johnny just stood there, staring at his magic hand, wondering what had gone wrong. And then it came to him. What had he been thinking? The florist shop had been closed since five o'clock that afternoon. There wasn't anyone inside. So it didn't matter that Johnny had himself a black fist that could work wonders. If there wasn't anyone behind the door to hear his knock, that five-fingered hunk of painted rubber was useless. Even a mojo hand couldn't command an empty building.

It took him awhile to get a hold of that idea. But once he got hold of it, he decided it didn't much matter. He'd lived in the real world for a long long time, and there were other tools at his disposal besides the mojo hand.

He went back to the truck and got two of them.

One was a .38, which he slipped behind him, under his belt, barrel along his spine.

The other was a cinder block.

Now, a lot of people in town didn't want anything to do with Johnny when he came marching home from the war. Ray Barnes was one of those.

Sheriff Ray Barnes, to be correct. Small-town cop going nowhere fast. Guy like that, of course he's going to have a hard-on for a war hero with a drawer full of medals. But Barnes wasn't prejudiced. He didn't much like *anyone*, and that made Halloween his favorite night of the year. People did stupid things, and Barnes made sure he was around when they did them. That's why the trunk of his cruiser was heavy with several cases of confiscated beer, courtesy of the town's teenage population. Up front, the sheriff had a bag of candy he'd snatched from some little window-soaper over at the church, even had the sawed-off runt's monster mask. Later tonight, Barnes figured he'd spook the little sweetheart over at dispatch with that mask. Make her jump right out of her skin.

But right now Barnes was chewing on one of the window-soaper's Hershey's bars and cruising the streets. That's the kind of guy he was. And that's why he got damn excited when a burglar alarm call directed him to a parking lot over on West Seventh. Because there was the war hero himself, Johnny Meyers, coming through the busted plate-glass door of the florist shop with an armful of roses, just as sweet as sweet could be.

Barnes grew a smile that was about half a yard wide. Everyone in town knew that Meyers was crackers, but the sheriff was the only one who was waiting to grind the soldier boy under his heel. Barnes hit the brakes. Ditched that Hershey's bar. Had his hand on his sidearm before he even released his seatbelt, which was a bitch to undo, but he did it.

His free hand found the door.

He was just about to open it when black rubber knuckles rapped the glass.

Hard. None of that *gently rapping, rapping at my chamber door* Eddie Poe stuff. This rap was loud enough to make Barnes' spine snap purely vertical. Then his head swiveled like a ventriloquist dummy's, and he saw Meyers standing right there at his side window, and the synapses in his miserable excuse for a brain fired off one serious barrage.

Barnes opened that car door double-quick.

Meyers didn't budge.

He held out an open hand. The one that wasn't rubber.

"Trick or treat, Sheriff," was all he said.

Goddamned if he knew why, but Barnes just couldn't help himself.

He put down his pistol.

He picked up a Snickers bar, and he placed it in Johnny Meyers' hand.

Johnny ate that Snickers as Barnes drove across town. He wasn't sure why he took the cop with him, but he did. The guy really was Johnny's to command. Barnes was as docile as a puppy. And with the burglar alarm going off back there, and Johnny's truck sitting smack dab in the middle of the parking lot—well, Johnny figured it wouldn't hurt to have the sheriff at his disposal should any other law come sniffing around.

Johnny thought things over as they drove. At least his mojo hand really worked. That was the good news, and Barnes proved it. But the bad news was that Johnny wasn't sure how many times he'd used his hand. He'd knocked on Barnes' squad car door, and that one surely counted. But he didn't know about the florist shop. He'd knocked there, too—only no one had answered. He had no way of knowing if that knock counted or not.

So maybe he'd used one knock, and maybe he'd used two. He'd planned to use that second knock over at the jewelry store, where he wanted to pick out a diamond ring for Elena. But that was going to have to wait. For one thing, he'd already set off one burglar alarm in town. For another, if there was only one knock left in that magic hand he had to save it for Elena's door…and for the man who answered it.

Familiar road now. Familiar moonlight, too. And through the cracked window, the familiar scent of the river and that dirt road still wet with rain that cut through farmland. And then that other smell—that crisp, tart apple smell that reminded Johnny of Elena's father.

It sliced straight through him like a knife. Johnny rolled up the window. Now all he could smell were the roses—the bouquet of white ones he'd managed to grab at the florist shop before Barnes showed up. He tried to settle in on it, but he had a hard time.

Johnny couldn't finish the Snickers bar. He tossed it back in the bag Barnes had stolen from a kid. Then he noticed something else in there. A monster mask, some kind of rattlesnake man with great big fangs. Johnny pulled it out and looked it over. Ran his hand over those scales. Rattlers were cold-blooded; they'd sleep through a night like this. They'd sleep through a whole damn winter. Johnny wished he could be that way, but he was sweating something fierce.

Barnes turned onto the little dirt road that led to Elena's house, and Johnny's heart started thundering. He was thinking about Elena's father, thinking how things would play out once the old man answered that door.

Barnes pulled to a stop.

Johnny swallowed hard.

He crumpled up that monster mask, shoved it into his coat pocket like a snakeskin charm.

He grabbed the white roses in his good hand.

He got out of the car and walked to the door.

He knocked.

It took a while before the door opened, but it did. And there stood Elena's father, his eyes tired, his heart heavy. Johnny told him what he wanted. But somehow, Johnny's words didn't seem to matter to the old man any more than Johnny's mojo hand mattered. Because Elena's father didn't have any more left in his heart or his house than he did in his words, and though he spoke them under the sway of Johnny's magic hand, they were words that did not rise above a whisper, and they were the same words that had knocked hard on Johnny's heart when he'd come home from the war three months before.

Johnny had denied those words entrance then, but he couldn't deny them now. Not as the three of them drove to the cemetery across the road from the apple orchard gone wild. The crisp, tart scent sawed at Johnny as he got out of the cruiser, and he remembered the things Elena's father had told him that day three months ago, and he recalled the details of a death that had come quietly while he was half a world away.

And now he remembered about the cemetery. And the smell of apples. And the scent of roses, too, for there were roses on Elena's grave. White roses...just like the ones he'd stolen from the florist shop. And suddenly Johnny felt like he was coming apart, felt like a busted puppet ready to topple among the tombstones.

He reached into his coat pocket. He squeezed that rattlesnake face in his good hand. Then he took the mask out of his pocket and put it on. He knew what he had to do.

Of course, a one-handed man couldn't use a shovel. Johnny didn't have time for that, anyway. So he started up the backhoe the gravediggers used and he set to work, digging like a combat knife in a tin of rations. Elena's father watched without a word. Ray Barnes watched too, chewing on a Snickers bar while he sat on a tombstone. And while Johnny worked the backhoe's gears, his stump of a wrist sweated inside the sleeve of his magic prosthetic hand, and his tears lined the inner skin of that rattlesnake mask.

But none of it mattered anymore. Not the mojo hand, not the white roses chewed under the teeth of the backhoe's bucket. Not what Johnny remembered, and not what he'd forgotten. That's what he thought as he emptied out that hole, and that's what he thought as he climbed down onto the lid of Elena's coffin with a dozen crushed roses and a rubber hand that had started off the evening swollen with the promise of three magic knocks.

One or none—how many magic knocks were left in that hand didn't matter at all. Johnny knew that deep inside, even as he held that rubber hand poised above the metal casket, even as he cried inside that rattlesnake mask.

Even as he brought his fist down on that lid.

And here's your kicker, folks—Johnny was right.

Because it doesn't really matter what happened next, any more than it matters why Johnny's hand was charged up with those three magic knocks in the first place. That's not what this story's about, because knocking on his dead love's coffin wasn't the worst thing that ever happened to Johnny Meyers. Not by a longshot.

The worst thing that ever happened to Johnny was ending up down in that hole at all.

The worst thing that happened was falling that deep, and that hard.

So…that's where Johnny is.

That's how he got there.

And that's where we'll leave him…tonight.

THE JACK O' LANTERN: A DARK HARVEST TALE

Cornstalks crackle as the October Boy shoulders into a small clearing. Moonlight fills that scooped hunk of the world, where stalks are rat-gnawed nubs trampled by a larger predator...a predator the Boy scents.

The scent is immediate. It hangs heavy as a shroud. The cool north wind combing the fields this Halloween night cannot banish it. The Boy's viney fingers twine tightly around the hilt of the butcher knife that fills his hand, as if he'll have to cut himself free of the stink before he can move so much as an inch.

But hesitation—real or imagined—is not a quality contained within the growing armature of the October Boy's body. He steps forward, his carved pumpkin head twisting on its braided-vine neck, beams of orange light spilling from his triangular eyes as he examines the shorn clearing.

There's a thing on the ground in the center of the circle. Another carved head, but one not like his own. Lanternlike, it burns. Flickering in the darkness, tongues of fire licking moisture within its hollowed confines. Casting a grinning shadowface that stretches across trampled stalks to the the Boy's severed-root feet. Spilling those predatory scents in this territory marked as his own, a stench that is nothing like the wild October scents of cool fall nights and cinnamon-laced gunpowder that have marked his birth and will mark his death.

The candy heart trapped in the Boy's woven chest beats faster as he travels the grinning map cast at his feet. He closes on the thing in the center of the circle. The shadowface gleams, its reflection contained on the polished surface of his blade as the Boy bends low. Yes, fire lives inside this carved head. Yes, the hollowed mouth spits moist crackles. Yes, a rabid grin spreads wider than any mouth can stretch, and its eyes are wells roiling with flame, and it is both exhibit and proof of a madman's art. But this strange Jack o' Lantern is nothing like a brother to the pumpkin-headed creature that holds the knife. This face—what remains of it—is not a carved product of the dark earth. It is a construct of flesh and bone. A human head, cored and hollowed—a half-dozen candles flickering within scraped red confines. Grinning a lipless grin over purple gums, a grin with bloodstained teeth rooted in a mouth that laughs no more.

But somewhere out there in the darkness, the October Boy hears laughter.

It lingers until it is eclipsed by another sound.

The sound of gunfire.

The Boy whirls away from the flickering Jack o' Lantern, but there's nothing out there to see but night, and stars, and the dull glow of the town waiting beyond.

He is alone in this clearing. The predator who lurked in this place is gone. Only the killer's trophy remains. In the end, this matters little to the October Boy, for tonight he too is a trophy. One that travels on two legs, destined to be slain if he makes a single misstep. One that knows this clearing is but a brief stop on a run that is a dead heat, with odds that never fall in his favor.

Another booming blast beckons him. And another. The October Boy cannot linger here, not if he wants a chance at staying alive. He is built for movement. This is what he must do to survive the human gauntlet that waits ahead in the night.

So the Boy turns his back, following his shadow away from the light cast by the mangled skull.

The black road waits.

A whisper through the corn, and he is on it.

Officer Dan Kehoe's scattergun barks, and lead shot clips the branches of an old cemetery oak. Barbed twigs and splinters rain down on a dozen boys fighting among the tombstones. They freeze, and Kehoe closes on them. They're bloody, rolling around among the granite slabs. Scratches and bruises and cuts on their faces. Ballbats and hammers and switchblades in their hands. Locked up and starved for five days. Mad with hunger. Free at last to hunt the October Boy, a scarecrow monster that hasn't even crossed the town limits yet.

In absence of that target, the boys turn on the only prey handy: each other. Kehoe understands that. Once, a long time ago, he was in their place—just another kid with dreams of winning the Run and escaping this nowhere town by killing a two-legged nightmare. Once, a long time ago, Kehoe's heart was a cage for the same fury that drives every young man between the ages of sixteen and nineteen this night.

Kill Sawtooth Jack and be the one guy to get out of here this year, or stay in this nowhere burg 'til your life rusts away to nothing. He remembers that promise as well as he understands it, and that is good. For even though every one of the kids in front of him is in twice the shape he is, and every one of them is a hundred times hungrier for a sweet piece of a life they can barely imagine, it's his job to direct their fury until the October Boy is brought down.

So Kehoe starts where the danger is, pile-driving the biggest kid into a tombstone. The boy is a straw-haired wideload armed with a pitchfork, and the dead man's marker catches him behind the knees and topples him like a dropped casket. The pitchfork flies out of the kid's hands as he falls. Quickly, Dan steps around the tombstone. His Winchester drives down as the boy tries to rise, butt plate digging into Wideload's thick muscled belly hard enough to jolt the kid's spine.

Guts, nerves, and muscle react. Wideload pukes up a bellyful of nothing on the cemetery lawn. But Kehoe isn't finished. A second later, the smoking shotgun barrel jams against the kid's cheek. Kehoe grabs Wideload's blond hair, jerking flushed skin tight against that hot steel so it's sure to leave a brand.

The boy whimpers, but Dan doesn't let go.

He's sending a message now.

He frosts the other boys with quick glances, one by one.

They stare at him, a man with close-cropped hair gone to gray. All those boys standing there, brains notching the distance between the reality they've just witnessed, the possible reactions it can trigger, and the likely price of those reactions. And then comes that one second. The only one Kehoe fears. The one where the boys might realize the odds aren't quite stacked in his favor. When they realized that Dan Kehoe is just one guy—an old guy, at that. And, sure, he wears a badge and he's armed with a shotgun, but there are a lot more of them than there are of him.

Dan studies their eyes, searching for a glimmer of that realization or the slightest twitch of muscle once it sparks. He sees neither. He's got them now, and he knows it. So he releases Wideload, chambering another shell before the kid moves so much as an inch.

Down on the ground, Wideload reaches for the scalded circle on his cheek. He swears under his breath, but he doesn't look Kehoe in the eye. Instead, he looks down, as if he's found a particularly interesting blade of grass planted between his knees.

That means one thing: it's over now. Kehoe knows it. He picks up the pitchfork, nudges it into the Wideload's hands. Then he points the shotgun at the cemetery gates.

"The Run's out there," Dan says. "So is the October Boy. Go get him, or I'll get you."

One blink, and the boys start moving.

Another, and they're already gone.

And that's when Dan Kehoe hears it. The squawk of the police radio, over in the prowl car parked by the cemetery gates. It's the chief. "Sounds like thunder out there," Steve Marlowe says. "That you, Dan?"

"Yeah. My shotgun, anyway. I just broke up a rumble in the cemetery. A bunch of kids trying to take each other apart instead of the Boy. Only one way to get those youngbloods on track."

"Twenty years ago, you wouldn't have needed the gun."

"Twenty years ago, I would have been kicking your ass, youngster."

Steve Marlowe laughs. The chief's pushing forty, but not too hard. And Kehoe's fifty-five.

"You seen Jack?" Marlowe asks.

"No," Kehoe says, because he has no idea where the other cop working the Run is. "What's up?"

"He said he was going to check the Line. That was more than an hour ago. Someone called in a tip about some jumpers. I've been trying to raise him for the last half hour, but all I get on the radio is dead air."

"Damn."

"How about you take a look out there?"

Kehoe swallows. The mic's right there in his hand. Open channel. His finger's perched over the button, but he can't think anything to say. He doesn't know why…or maybe he does. Maybe that moment is still eating at him—the moment when he waited for those youngblood's to react. Or maybe it's the sudden quiet that's fallen over the cemetery. Maybe it's the simple fact that he's sitting here, all alone among the tombstones in the quietest place in town. Knowing what's right here, six feet under his boot heels.

Yeah. Maybe that's it. Because for some reason Dan Kehoe can't quite understand, tonight he's feeling closer to that boxed and buried stretch of real estate than he does to the streets of this town, or the kids running those streets, or the October Boy. Call it instinct if you want. Or call it premonition, maybe. But the feeling churning in Kehoe's gut is definite if not quite definable, and—

"You still there, Dan?"

"You really want me heading out of town, Chief? If the Run hits rough water without a cop on the streets, you're up shit creek."

"Could be I'm already there."

"What are you saying, boss?"

"I'm saying I want you to find my other badge before the water gets too deep…and I want you to do it now."

Walking the black road is like walking a prison corridor. Dead cornstalks rise like a crop of iron bars on each side of the asphalt, leading toward the only real cage the October Boy has ever known.

The town. The Boy moves toward it, wondering if he's walking his first mile or his last. If he beats the odds and makes it to the old brick church before midnight, then this is his first mile. If he fails, then it could be his last.

And once he crosses the Line that separates the town from the fields, every step he takes will be a hundred times more dangerous than the ones he's taking now. He raises his head as screams rise in the distance. Howls and roars spill from the mouths of hungry boys who'll hunt him this night. The October Boy understands his pursuers just as Dan Kehoe understands them, for he has traveled in their shoes. He knows the fate they plan for him is no different than the fate suffered by that hacked-up head in the clearing—a living thing severed from that role by a murderous hand…now no more than an object.

But the Boy cannot dwell on such things. And, when it comes to fate, he has a knife of his own—one he will use this night to carve his own quotient of same.

So he moves on, blade at the ready. The screams in the distance trail off. The road stretches ahead, a licorice whip even when washed in moonlight. Suddenly it's quiet here…almost. Only the whisper of the October Boy's feet on asphalt. Only the croaking of frogs in the deep ditches at the side of the road.

And now the Boy spots something just ahead…something in that ditch…something much too large that the moonlight paints the same way it paints the road. The Boy's carved eyes narrow, and the orange glow spilling from his head brightens as Atomic Fireballs crackle in his skull. His gaze spotlights the center-line of the road until it slices over the body of a car.

The car is black.

The car is white.

It's two-tone: a police cruiser.

The Boy freezes, remembering the severed head in the field. The predatory scent is gone, but perhaps there is a greater danger here. The prowl car door hangs open. There's another crackle, and this one is not contained in the Boy's skull. It's the police radio, but no one's there to answer it.

The Boy can see that. The cruiser's interior fills with orange light as he draws near. He fears a trap, but the road is empty, and the cornstalks do not rustle. The wind has suddenly died. The frogs are quiet. He's sure he is alone…at least for the moment.

The Boy ducks his misshapen head inside the prowl car. He may not have long. But no keys hang from the ignition. He exhales hard, hot breath scalding his crosscut excuse for a smile. He'll have no shortcut into town tonight. It will not be so easy.

But there's something else there in the car. Not the thing he thought he'd find, but something he can use.

The Boy buries his butcher knife in the driver's seat, making a trade.

In a second, he has a Winchester Model 97 shotgun in his hands.

Quickly, he fills the pockets of his tattered coat with spare shells. A V8 guns in the distance, and the Boy senses it's the same big block engine he'd find under the prowl car's hood if he gave it a pop.

A half-mile away, headlights drill through the night. By the time those lights reveal the abandoned police cruiser, the October Boy is already gone.

He's cutting through the dead corn, a shotgun in his hands.

Kehoe stares at the butcher knife buried at spine-level in the driver's seat of Jack's squad car. That familiar fear churns low in his gut, so thoroughly he doesn't even notice the missing shotgun.

Because he's alone here on the black road, just the way he was in the cemetery.

Or maybe he's not alone at all.

After all, this is someone else's territory. Someone he remembers very well. The October Boy. It's been more than thirty-five years since Dan was part of the Run, thirty since he became a cop and separated its truths from its lies, but fear of the Boy is hard-wired in everyone who grew up in this town. Sawtooth Jack...Ol' Hacksaw Face...whatever you call him, you never completely shake that primal terror or the adrenaline that makes it pump. Not really. Not even when you're clear of your eighteenth year.

It's always with you—especially if you stand out here on the black road, alone under the stars. Especially if you catch the odd stink of scorched cinnamon, gunpowder, and melted wax lingering on the night air. Yeah. The October Boy's been here, all right. Kehoe's sure of that. And now a squad car sits empty on the far side of the Line, and a cop is missing.

It's Kehoe's job to find him. He steps away from the car, shines a flashlight down the licorice whip two-lane. "Jack!" Kehoe calls. "Jack! You out there?"

No answer.

Kehoe starts down the road, feeling like there's a black cat squirming in his belly. He keeps his eyes on the corn, wary that a pumpkin-headed thing is going to rush from the fields and try to kill him...maybe just the way it killed Jack.

But even as Kehoe walks, a calmer part of his brain works over that idea. It doesn't make sense, not when you consider it within the parameters of this night. The Run is a young man's game. The Boy only hunts those between the ages of sixteen and nineteen. They're the ones he's looking for, because they're looking for him, too. Kehoe's never heard of the Boy tangling with a cop, let alone murdering one.

And, hell, Jack's as old as Kehoe. He's no kid. He's got a son of his own. His boy tried to shoehorn a spot on the force last year. Just twenty-two, and already pushing to get a badge. As if his old man and Kehoe were ready for pensions and retirement and the quiet that comes when you aren't part of the Harvester's Guild machine anymore, when all that's left for you is to sit back at night and let the things you did and didn't do in your life eat at your guts.

No man needs that. Not Kehoe, anyway. He doesn't want to retire. Do that and he might as well put a down-payment on a pine box. Just like the October Boy, Dan Kehoe needs to keep moving to stay alive. That's why he's still out here tonight. And that's why Jack got his kid a job over at the slaughterhouse. Jack doesn't want to slow down, either. Told his kid to bide his time, wait for his own moment. Told him he needed to learn to butcher animals before he learned how to butcher—

There's a light up ahead, flickering low in the corn.

Too low to be the October Boy.

Still, Kehoe eases his .38 from the holster. Cocks it. Steps through the brittle stalks without another word. A dead man's skull waits in a trampled clearing. Flames where its eyes should be, because a half-dozen candles fill the hollow place that once housed its brain. Flickering sockets gleam over half a face that's just plain gone, sliced into a wide naked smile that stretches ear to ear, revealing gums and teeth still wet with blood.

Kehoe recognizes the face, of course—even if it's one that never smiled much.

It belongs to a cop he's worked with for thirty years.

A man named Jack Ricks.

Jack Ricks' son drives through town, a blood-stained butcher knife on the car seat at his side. No one's supposed to be on the road, of course. But young Jerry Ricks isn't exactly worried about getting a ticket. Thanks to that bloody butcher knife, one cop—his own father—is dead. By now, Jerry's sure that another cop—Dan Kehoe—is staring at what's left of Daddy's corpse. Jerry plans to deal with ol' Dan before the night is through. As far as Jerry's concerned, Officer Kehoe has written his last ticket.

Tonight it's time to get that ticket punched. That'll happen soon enough. A grin creases Jerry's thin face. He hammers the gas, laughing as those Goodyears peel. Daddy's dead and ol' Dan's occupied. That only leaves one other cop in this one-horse town—and Jerry knows exactly where Chief Steve Marlowe is at.

Fact is, he's on his way to see the chief right now.

Marlowe's voice crackles over the radio as Dan Kehoe's story settles in. "So you think it was the Boy?"

Kehoe thumbs the mic. "Everything points that way. Or seems to...but it doesn't make sense. It's been a long time since any of us were eighteen. We're not exactly the Boy's meat. And Jack wouldn't get in the Boy's way—he knows that a kid has to bring down ol' Hacksaw Face on the night of the Run or this whole town might as well get shoveled in a bucket."

"Maybe the Boy's just hard for anything wearing a badge," Marlowe says. "You factor in how he ended up in the game tonight, I wouldn't blame him for that. I think we'd better tag-team this action. Get over to the station and pick me up. We'll figure out what's gone wrong with that monster."

"Will do," Kehoe says. "But I'm making a stop first."

"Where?"

"Jack's house. We should check on his kid. He and the old man had their troubles. The level of violence we're looking at, we've got to consider there was some strong emotion cooking here. I want to know that Jack's kid is exactly where he belongs before we go any further."

"Look, Dan. We don't have time to play hunches tonight—"

But Kehoe has already cut the radio.

Now he hits the gas.

They're twenty feet away when they glimpse the October Boy's glowing face in the cornfield on the edge of town. Six boys, football players from the freshman class. Armed with axe handles, ballbats…one kid with a machete.

They charge as one.

They haven't noticed the shotgun. Spitting laughter that stinks of gunpowder and scorched cinnamon, the October Boy whips it up—but not too high. One quick pump and he lets loose. Shot splatters in front of the charging pack, and the load kicks off the blacktop, hitting the boys low, shredding blue jeans and chewing like hungry metal ticks into the young flesh beneath.

Two of the boys go down instantly. The October Boy jacks the slide handle, chambering another shell as the mob swallows its first collective taste of real fear. He fires again, and suddenly they're not a mob anymore. Now they're only targets, and scattering ones at that.

Hollow laughter spills over the Boy's carved smile. The sound sweeps the boys down the street like a gigantic broom. The October Boy squints tightly, tracking them with the shotgun, one tendril finger quite literally twined around the trigger while his spotlight eyes gleam from rear bead to front. But he doesn't pull that trigger. Not now. Not when he's got six backsides in his sites, growing smaller in the distance.

No. He'll save his shells. Tonight he'll need them, sure enough. He looks around. There's nothing behind him in the field. For the moment, this little street on the north side of town is empty.

But he'll have to move fast, because word will spread just that way now that he's crossed the Line. Soon everyone will know he's entered town with a shotgun. By the time that knowledge becomes common, the Boy hopes it will be too late to do his pursuers any good. If things go right he'll be close to the heart of town by then, cutting a zigzag path to the church that marks his finish line. Pulling that trigger when he has to, killing when he must.

This is what the Boy thinks as he advances into town, severed-root feet sweeping over pockmarked blacktop where six boys have spilled blood.

He turns down an alley that'll trim two long blocks off his journey.

He slips into the darkest shadows.

And finds that he is already there.

Jerry Ricks stands at the back door of the police station. The door is metal—reinforced steel—but Jerry has his father's key. Chief Marlowe is the only man inside. Outside, in the alley, it's just Jerry and the October Boy.

Jerry's fingers are closed around the key, but he doesn't give it a twist. It's a strange moment. There's a bloody butcher knife in his other hand, and a rubber pumpkin mask on his face. It's the same mask he wore when he surprised his father earlier that night and murdered him out in the cornfield.

Jerry can't help it. He shivers at the sight of the only bogeyman he's ever feared. The October Boy stares at him, spotlighting Jerry's rubber mask with Halloween eyes, raising a shotgun like a poised gavel of eternity. As the gun sweeps up the Boy's gaze drifts lower, to the blood-stained blade in Jerry's hand.

The October Boy pauses.

His eyes narrow to slivers.

A crosscut mistake of a smile arches high on his face.

And just that fast, laughter spills from the Boy's head—the same dark laughter that a few minutes before swept a half-dozen boys off a street just like a broom. It's a sardonic laugh brimming with realization, but it doesn't scare Jerry Ricks. No. It infuriates him. His fear is suddenly gone. He won't have this thing laughing at him like he's some pretender to its dark throne. Because he knows what the October Boy is, and what he isn't. He's not like those kids running the streets tonight—the ones who think the nightmarish scarecrow is a ticket to a dream.

No. Standing there in a frightmask of his own, Jerry knows better. He understands the truth. There is no escape from this town. The Run is a self-fullfilling prophecy, and so is the Boy, and so are those who long for that fabled one-way ticket across the Line. Because what would Jerry have gained if he'd been one of the kids who brought down the Boy and earned a trip on the black road, anyway? Not a one-way ticket out of this dead-end little nowhere. Just a detour to a hole in the ground—and without the benefit of a pine box.

Once Jerry thought it was different. He didn't understand that winning the Run meant having worms chew your corpse through a long winter and spring and summer, or coming back to the same damn town a year later with a twisted body and a knife in your hands. But now he understands everything. It's all about lies here. Lies his father told him. Lies every father told. Lies about the town, and the Run, and the October Boy himself.

Lies about death, and—even worse—lies about life.

The way Jerry sees it, the biggest lie of all stands in front of him with a shotgun. The October Boy's eyes burn brightly, as if Jerry's fate is cooking around in its brainpan and the clock is just a handful of ticks from dinnertime. Like everything else around here, the Boy wants blood. Ricks understands that, because he wants blood, too. Blood washes away every lie. Blood is how you pay your way in this town. With the Boy. With the Harvester's Guild. And even with your own family.

Jerry smiles behind his mask. Yes. Blood is the only currency that counts around here, and it's all about paying the price.

Jerry raises his butcher knife. The Boy jacks a load into the shotgun chamber, but Jerry doesn't hesitate. He steps forward. Inside his Jack o' Lantern mask, he laughs a laugh all his own. It's higher than he wants, and it bottles up inside the mask as if it has nowhere to go, and he can't control the way it spills from his lips any more than he can control the blade of the knife.

That honed hunk of stainless steel gleams as it opens a quick, sure slice along the heel of Jerry Ricks' palm. He flicks his hand toward the Boy. Blood splatters the alley. It rains over blacktop. A fat drop hits a garbage can, and another the brick wall behind it, and another still a window smoked with grime.

Another kick of his hand, and his blood slaps the October Boy's tattered coat.

Another flick. And another…and another…

"You want more?" the masked killer asks. "Is that what you want?"

He's descending the cement stairs at the rear of the police station, sweeping his cut hand before him, spraying blood across the alley.

"A cup gonna do you? A pint? A quart?"

Blood splatters the ground at the October Boy's gnarled feet.

"Is that enough for you? Let me know, Boy. Because I'll give you all you want. I'll give you all you can handle."

The October Boy's arrowhead nose flares to a tighter point. He holds his ground, even though the wild red stink chokes him. How could he have missed it when he entered the alley? It's the same predator's scent that he smelled in the clearing where he found the severed head.

And now the killer who carved that trophy is heading his way. A cold wind travels with him, filling the narrow brick tunnel, tumbling newspapers and trash, moving the black around. But it does nothing to dispel the murderous stench, or the blood splattering the Boy in Rorschach droplets, or the orange beam of light that connects the Boy's gaze to the killer's raised knife.

The Boy levels his shotgun, but the killer doesn't slow his step.

The masked thing only laughs, sending another shower of blood across the alley.

"Sawtooth Jack," the killer says. "That's what they call you. I'll give you all you can take, Jack. I'll give you a bellyful."

The bloody hand flicks again. Blood slaps the October Boy's carved face. A drop flies between his teeth and he tastes its bitter salt. And now, his anger rises. Because no one can tell him about blood, or what it's for, or what it costs. Especially not a pretender who hides behind a rubber face that's a mockery of his own. The October Boy doesn't have a single drop of red in him anymore, but he knows all about blood. He spilled every drop he could spare last year in that cornfield where a cop put a bullet in his brain. Now he's just a rooted thing that doesn't bleed, a thing bred by photosynthesis and sunlight and the cursed light of the moon, a thing fed by the dark earth whose roots are now severed and dying at the tips of his twisted feet.

"C'mon," the killer says, because he understands none of that. "We both know how this game is played. Hell, I've worked in a slaughterhouse for the last year. I've spilled blood. I've washed my hands in it. I'd drink it straight from the vein if that's what it took to get what I want. And I'll give it up, too. I'll give as much as I need to get everything I want."

Another red gout flies through the air, but this time it doesn't reach the October Boy. Stoked fire flares in his carved head, and the alley lights up with angry flame. That spray of blood sizzles to ash in midair, long before it can touch the Boy.

A second later, slivers of ash drift to the ground. That stops the maniac cold. The fire in the Boy's head remains a stoked, banked glow. He steadies the shotgun, backing off slowly, but he knows he won't pull the trigger. The report of his weapon would be too high a price for killing this maniac. Instantly, every boy in town would know where he was.

And now the Boy speaks, his sandpaper voice scraping the silence.

"We'll settle this," the Boy says. "Another night."

The words are a promise. And now that the promise has been scorched on the night, this is no place to linger.

The October Boy doesn't.

Kehoe parks in front of a little house on North Harvest Street. Scrabby lawn, paint peeling. Jack Ricks hadn't really taken care of the place since his wife died two years ago.

Of course, Jack hadn't taken care of what was inside the house, either. Hadn't gotten along with his boy, Jerry, for a good long time. They tussled and then some. Especially when Jerry started pushing to be a cop, when anyone who could read the writing on the wall knew there were only so many guys in town that the Guild slotted for the job each generation. But Jerry didn't want to wait his turn, and now Kehoe is almost positive it's led to this—slaughterhouse patricide out in a cornfield, a job done by a kid who definitely had plenty of experience with the tools of the trade.

That's the way Dan sees it, anyway. Hell, he's spent thirty years peeling away secrets in this town and learning how to add them up. And Dan's learned something else during that time: you manage to stick around a lot longer in this town if you work things out with a gun in your hand.

He gets out of the car, .38 drawn, approaching the house as if he's walking into a meat-grinder. The drapes are drawn. There's a frosted-glass window in the door, and a patch of dull light behind it. Kehoe gives the knob a twist. It's open. He eases inside, closing the door behind him.

The house is quiet. Unless they're on Guild business or wearing a badge, everyone who's over the age of eighteen should be inside tonight. And there's no sign of Jerry here…which means the younger Mr. Ricks certainly isn't playing things the way he should.

Kehoe moves down the hallway leading to Jerry's room. There are no pictures on the walls, but that doesn't surprise Dan. There isn't a family in this house. Just two men jockeying for one life. He opens the bedroom door and turns on the light. Nothing much in there but a low stale reek. Slaughterhouse clothes on the floor. A bed without sheets and a balled up sleeping bag on the mattress. A couple empty orange juice jugs. A butcher knife on the table, and a bunch of brown, peeled apples in a garbage can on the floor. As if Jack's son had been starving himself for the last five days, drinking nothing but OJ while he peeled apples he wasn't going to eat, torturing himself the way some of the hard-core town jocks do to get themselves geared up for the Run.

The smell of slaughterhouse blood and rotting apples makes Dan's gut churn.

He hears a creak. Outside. Somewhere in the back yard.

He whirls toward the door, steps into the hallway, pausing just a moment and—

That creak again.

Quickly, deliberately, Kehoe moves into the living room. He follows the barrel of his .38 through the dining room and into the kitchen. The back window faces a covered patio. There's something out there in the moonlight. A twist of shadows and it moves.

Creak.

Kehoe's free hand is already on the doorknob.

The back door flies open.

Dan steps outside, pistol leveled at the thing.

A held breath escapes him. Hanging from the patio overhang is a heavy bag. The kind boxers use. Kehoe sees that now, and the sight triggers a memory. Dan remembers nights he's worked the graveyard shift, spotting Jerry Ricks out on the streets doing roadwork, as if Jerry were training for a fight when there are no fights to train for around here but the ones you can never quite win—

Out on North Harvest, a car door slams.

Footsteps click along the sidewalk, turn up the front walk.

"Shit," Kehoe whispers.

He's back in the house in a second, heading for the front door with that .38 in his hand.

The farm boy drives a pitchfork forward, catching the October Boy hard, pinning his right leg against a big boat of a black sedan.

The shotgun thunders. The farm boy drops. The Boy jacks another shell into the chamber. Others are coming. Two kids dressed in black, closing from the movie theater on Main Street. The Boy's right hand vines around the slide handle and the shotgun barrel. The blue steel is so hot it's scorching his tendril fingers, but he ignores the pain.

He fires again. Lead shot tatters leather jackets and the flesh beneath. Blood spills. Boys go down. For just a moment, nothing moves in the darkness. The October Boy glances up Main Street. There's the brick church, just a few hundred yards away. If he can just get free of the pitchfork, he can make it. If only this moment will last a little longer—

But it can't last. The Boy knows that. In the distance, Chuck Taylors whisper on asphalt. Shadows spill beneath streetlights on Main, stretching across brick and glass and sidewalk.

The boys are getting ready for another assault. It won't be long before they come at him again. The Boy knows this. He has to free himself, and he has to do it now. He leans the shotgun against the car, and his fingers twine around the pitchfork's steel shafts. He yanks at it…then he yanks again, sucking a hard breath that flares the stoked fire in his head—

A bitter tang fills his mouth. The harsh perfume of gasoline. The Boy looks down, sees that the pitchfork has pinned him near the sedan's gas cap. One of the tines has pierced the capped line. And now that he's trying to free himself, a thin stream of gas is pumping from the tank. It's trickling down the side of the car, dripping on the ground at his feet—

The Boy yanks again. The pitchfork won't budge.

A taut whisper from the shadows across the street, and an arrow shatters the car window just inches from the Boy's arm.

Another arrow cuts the night, striking the Boy in the chest.

A third pierces the knotted coil of creepers that form his right shoulder.

And now they're coming again. Fast. Four kids in letterman's jackets. The Boy's carved head swivels up, orange streams of light revealing eyes as dark as the madman's blood that stains the October Boy's clothes. The streets are heavy with the stink of it. The young men jump puddles spilled by the October Boy's victims, vaulting dead bodies as if they're no more than sacks of grain.

They don't care about anything that's dead. Not tonight. They only care about their quarry, and they're closing on him now.

The Boy can only watch them come. At the front of the pack, there's another kid with a pitchfork. He's big, with a shock of cornhusk hair and a circular brand on one cheek.

He's close now, as close as he needs to be. One grunt, and his pitchfork flies through the air. In a second, it will split the Boy's head wide open.

For the October Boy, it doesn't matter.

Once again, the shotgun fills his hands.

The barrel points down at a thin puddle of spreading gasoline.

The Boy stares at the church as the pitchfork hits him.

He pulls the trigger.

Gasoline ignites.

A moment later, all that remains is fire.

Kehoe's near the front door, his back to the wall, the .38 cocked and ready.

The door whispers open. The first thing through it is a shotgun barrel, guided by a pair of gloved hands. Dan is just a foot away, but he'd have to holster his pistol to make a grab for the scattergun. No way he'll do that. Instead, he'll wait…just a second…until the intruder has entered the room.

The man moves on, his face pushing at shadows as he passes. It's grotesque. Black eyes. Ridges of orange skin. A Jack o' Lantern grin. For an instant, Kehoe is certain it's the Boy himself. Then he smells the rubber mask. He grabs the back of it, twists it to the side so the guy inside can't see anything. Then he hammers him with the butt of the .38.

The shotgun clatters to the floor. Kehoe shucks that mask like it's a cornhusk as the intruder goes down. Dan jams the .38's barrel against Jerry Ricks' sweaty face as soon as Ricks plants his knees on the floorboards.

"You almost had me," Kehoe says. " Almost."

He pushes Jerry forward, dropping him on all fours while he kicks the shotgun across hardwood floor. Dan presses the pistol barrel against the back of Ricks' head. He's done this kind of thing before. Many times. Out there in the cornfield where the Run's winners are put down. Other places, too. It's how the old take care of the young around here—the ones who never learn to toe the line.

And that's the way it is with Jack Ricks' boy. He's much too dangerous to live. "You thought you were smart," Kehoe tells him. "Thought you'd take out your old man. Take me out, too. Blame both killings on the October Boy and get a badge pinned to your chest just that quick. Too bad it's not going to work out that way."

"It's the only way it can work out," Ricks says.

"You're wrong about that, Jerry. You should have paid attention to how things work around here. You should have waited your turn."

"Waiting your turn is just waiting to die."

Kehoe's fury rises. The .38 whips out before he knows it. He hits Ricks again, and the kid crumples. A thin line of blood spills from his scalp. Dan hears it strike the floor, very softly, drop by drop.

"That was a good one," Ricks says, almost laughing now. "That almost did the job."

"Jobs only get done one way around here, boy. Your daddy should have taught you that a long time ago."

Kehoe cocks the .38.

He feels the pressure of another pistol against his neck.

"Drop the gun, Dan," Steve Marlowe says. "And do it now."

And now it's Kehoe's turn. Marlowe stands in front of him with a .38. Young Jerry Ricks is at the chief's side with that Winchester shotgun leveled at Dan's chest.

And no one really needs to say anything. Least of all Dan Kehoe. Seeing the look in Marlowe's eyes, the events of this night makes perfect sense now. It's just another changing of the guard. Different than the one that happens every year around here when the October Boy makes his Run to nowhere and is replaced by a corpse who'll take his place the following year, but inevitable in just the same way.

One young Chief of Police who wants things done his way. Two older cops who maybe do things their own way a little too often, who maybe have lost a step or two over the years. One young and eager recruit, crazy enough to do anything he's told as long as he gets to trade a life hacking up beef-on-the-hoof for one where he gets to do pretty much the same thing to human beings while wearing a badge.

Yeah. That's how it plays out here tonight. Kehoe knows it, the same way he knows the way the story will spread tomorrow. *"Did you hear the news? The October Boy killed Jack Ricks and Dan Kehoe last night. Cut off Ricks' head out in the cornfield, then stole a shotgun from Jack's prowl car. Once he crossed the Line, he put so much buckshot in Kehoe that he chopped the old hardcase in half. Hell of a thing...but at least it looks like young Jerry Ricks is going to take his old man's place. They'll keep that badge in the family. Marlowe's swearing him in this morning. Too bad Kehoe didn't have himself a son...."*

Uh-huh. That's the way it will go. Dan sucks a deep breath. There's not much left now, but his mind keeps working it over. There's really nothing else to do.

And it's funny where his mind takes him in those last seconds of life. Funny. He remembers other moments just like this one, out in the cornfield. He remembers boys down on their knees in front of his gun. Sixteen years old...or seventeen, or eighteen. He thinks of all the years he had that they never got. And he remembers that single moment when this night was younger, out there in the cemetery when he was all alone, feeling the pull of those boxes that wait beneath the ground.

All those years he had in between. All those years—

Jerry Ricks jacks a load into the shotgun.

"Nothing personal, Dan," Steve Marlowe says. "It's just hell to get old."

Of course, the candles in his father's skull have long since burned out by the time Jerry revisits the cornfield with Chief Marlowe. They're in a different clearing this time. This year's winner is down on his knees. Jerry has a .38 in his hand. The kid who brought down the October Boy is big—he looks like a football player. His clothes are scorched, and so is his blond hair—it's as if the kid slaughtered the October Boy in a blast furnace or something. Even weirder, the guy has a circle branded on one cheek. Jerry wonders how he got it...but he doesn't wonder too hard.

After all, he's got work to do.

It starts with a gun, and it ends with a shovel.

The Chief says, "You did all right tonight, kid."

Jerry says, "Yeah."

They're alone now, just the two of them out in the cornfield. Just them and that dead boy at their feet, and a hole in the ground that's waiting to become his cradle.

Jerry has a shovel. Marlowe has a couple of badges. He hands them over.

"Souvenirs," he says. "You get your own tomorrow."

"Sure," Jerry says, pinning the badges to his shirt.

Marlowe grins, then turns his back and walks away. He's almost to the edge of the clearing when he stops in a patch of moonlight. "One other thing," he says.

"Yeah, Chief?"

"You work for the Harvester's Guild now, Jerry. And that means there's only one rule: we'll take care of you…as long as you take care of this town."

Jerry doesn't hesitate.

"I can do that, Chief," he says. "For a long, long time."

And it's strange how the night stretches out, expanding to contain all the work that needs to be done. Jerry Ricks gets busy. Digging that grave a little deeper. Rolling this year's winner into it. Filling it in—working that shovel so his back feels the pure hurt of it, not to mention his bandaged hand.

It's bleeding again—that cut he made when he stood face-to-face with the October Boy. The stained gauze is wet with rust-colored grime, and now and again a drop falls at Jerry's feet or into the open grave. He leans on the shovel for a minute, and he watches one drop descend into the black hole, and then another, and he almost feels like he travels with them.

No lie. He sure enough took a test-drive through the darkness tonight. But Jerry doesn't worry about that. In a way, it hardly seems real, all the things he's done. It's like all the things around here that no one ever talks about. All those things that happen and get shoveled into a thousand black holes.

And it doesn't matter anyway. In a few more hours the sun will rise, and the night will move off somewhere else. A few more weeks, and Jerry's wounded hand will heal. That's the way it always is around here. The darkness opens up, and it pulls you down inside for a while. And you do what you need to do while it wraps you up in there, and then you crawl back once you've earned your time in the light. And sure, you spill some blood... but in the end you stitch up your wounds, and your skin scars over. And that's just the way it is.

Everyone has scars.

Everyone around here, anyway.

Jerry knows that. He stares down in the hole. He wonders about that hunk of dead meat down there—he imagines it's the one thing around here with wounds that never truly scar over. He wonders, too, if it's already starting to change. Three feet of dirt on top of that corpse already. Another couple feet of good topsoil to go before Jerry tamps it down and turns his back on this night, leaving next year's October Boy alone in a dirty cradle where it will sprout, and grow, and strain toward the light.

Jerry snatches the shovel from the earth. He gets busy again, scooping that topsoil, listening to the wind rustling through the corn. It's a sound like sandpaper working over the night, scraping it down to the rising dawn. Jerry can almost hear the Boy's voice in it—those same words that crossed his hacksaw grin just hours ago.

"We'll settle this," the Boy says. "Another night."

That's okay with Jerry.

He'll be waiting.

He's going exactly nowhere.